Brie asked.

Shoving his hat to the back of his head, Drew grinned. "Yeah, I guess so."

"Then allow me to make myself perfectly clear. My answer is no. When—and *if*—I marry, it will be for love and nothing less."

"But this marriage would only be temporary."

Well, of course it would be temporary, Brie told herself. Certainly, she expected nothing more from him. After all, he was a temporary kind of guy. Here today, gone tomorrow. A woman would be a fool to think otherwise.

Dear Reader,

Silhouette Romance rings in the New Year with a great new FABULOUS FATHER from bestselling author Elizabeth August! Murdock Parnell may be the *Ideal Dad* for eight-year-old Jeremy Galvin, but will he convince Jeremy's pretty mom, Irene, that he's her ideal husband?

In Kristin Morgan's latest book, Brianna Stansbury is *A Bride To Be*. Problem is, her groom-to-be is up to no good. It's up to Drew Naquin to rescue Brianna—even if that means marrying her himself!

Expectant Bachelor concludes Sandra Steffen's heartwarming WEDDING WAGER series about three brothers who vow they'll never say "I do." This time, Taylor Harris must battle the forces of love. And once he discovers the woman in his arms plans to be the mother of his child, it's not easy.

Rounding out the month, Carol Grace brings us a *Lonely Millionaire* who's looking for a mail-order bride. Liz Ireland turns up the laughter when a young woman finds herself playing *Mom for a Week*—with only her long-ago love to rescue her. And look for *The Man Who Changed Everything* from debut author Elizabeth Sites.

Until next month,

Happy reading!

Anne Canadeo
Senior Editor

Please address questions and book requests to:
Silhouette Reader Service
U.S.: 3010 Walden Ave., P.O. Box 1325, Buffalo, NY 14269
Canadian: P.O. Box 609, Fort Erie, Ont. L2A 5X3

A BRIDE TO BE

Kristin Morgan

Silhouette

R O M A N C E™

Published by Silhouette Books

America's Publisher of Contemporary Romance

To Jessica and Ro,
whose friendships I treasure

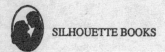 SILHOUETTE BOOKS

ISBN 0-373-19055-7

A BRIDE TO BE

Copyright © 1995 by Barbara Lantier Veillon

Printed in U.S.A.

Books by Kristin Morgan

Silhouette Romance

KRISTIN MORGAN

lives in Lafayette, Louisiana, the very heart of Acadiana, where the French language of her ancestors is still spoken fluently by her parents and grandparents. Happily married to her high school sweetheart, she has three children. She and her husband have traveled all over the South, as well as other areas of the United States and Mexico, and they both count themselves lucky that their favorite city, New Orleans, is only two hours away from Lafayette.

In addition to her writing, she enjoys cooking and preparing authentic Cajun foods for her family with recipes passed on to her through the generations. Her hobbies include reading—of course!—flower gardening and fishing. She loves walking in the rain, newborn babies, all kinds of music, chocolate desserts and love stories with happy endings. A true romantic at heart, she believes all things are possible with love.

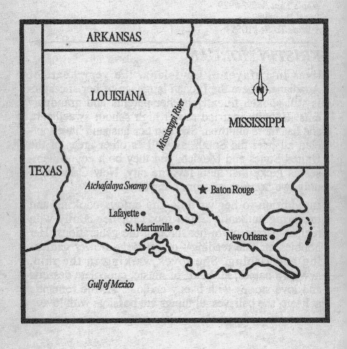

Chapter One

So in the end, this was where a treasure hunter went when he died. It seemed anticlimactic—almost sad—considering the adventurous life he'd led.

Brie Stansbury gazed in silence at the freshly dug grave she'd been directed to by the groundskeeper of the old, though sparsely populated little cemetery. Someone, she supposed the uninterested-looking caretaker with whom she'd spoken, had carelessly tossed a couple of floral wreaths, now dried and faded after a week in the hot sun, on top of the dirt-covered mound. Brie placed her bouquet of fresh white daisies wrapped in green tissue paper between the two wreaths and then dropped her hands to her sides. She'd thought she would cry at this point, but tears didn't come. Maybe, she decided, because she'd already cried enough. She'd had six days to recover from the shock of learning her grandfather had died after an extended illness with cancer. In truth, she hadn't even known he was sick.

Suddenly tears that had been slow in coming sprang to Brie's eyes.

There was no use in trying to pretend that she wasn't hurt by this final rejection from her grandfather, because she was. She felt betrayed. Not only had she been kept unaware of his illness, but she had also learned that it was because of *his* request that she'd received the news of his death too late for her to make it across four state lines to attend his funeral. She was his only grandchild, for heaven's sake. Actually, his only living relative. She should have been there. She *would have* been there, had she known in time.

A choking sob escaped Brie's throat as she suddenly realized her continuous struggle to win her grandfather's love was finally over. And she had lost.

Feeling the sorrow of her defeat, she dropped her head and allowed her tears to fall to the ground. But after a few moments, she inhaled deeply, lifted her tear-streaked face to the pale blue sky overhead and slowly regained her composure. She told herself that undoubtedly it was for the best that she'd received the news of his death too late to attend his funeral service. Otherwise, she would have had to deal with the added emotional stress of meeting all of his friends and acquaintances, people whose names and faces were completely foreign to her, and that would only have emphasized the fact that she'd never been an active, necessary part of his life.

In actuality, if she had come for his services, she would only have known one person in attendance, and he was Drew Naquin, her grandfather's young associate. Drew Naquin, whom she'd met once nine years ago. Most likely he was the one who had taken charge of making all the final arrangements for the wake and funeral—arrangements that should have been hers to make. With regard to

Mr. Naquin, however, she had no regrets. Even today, with all her emotional guards in place, Brie wasn't sure she was ready to see him again.

If the truth were told, she didn't know if she ever would be. Not after the fool she'd made of herself all those years ago when her grandfather had brought him along on one of his rare visits to her home in Atlanta. She'd grown up a lot since then—emotionally, anyway—and Drew Naquin probably wasn't going to recognize the woman she'd become. For one thing, she didn't wear her feelings on her sleeve anymore.

In fact, today, at the age of twenty-six, it didn't really matter to her that she'd once had a childish crush on him. Nor did it matter that he'd been very much aware of that fact on that warm summer night so long ago when she'd naively asked him to kiss her and, instead, he'd turned his back and walked away. She had been humiliated, shattered by that experience, but she had gotten over it. It didn't even bother her when, over the course of the next few years, she came to the realization that he—a complete stranger—meant more to her grandfather than she ever would. No, sirree, today, none of that mattered.

And even if it had, it was too late to change anything. She was here in Lafayette, Louisiana, simply because the attorney who had telephoned her with the news of her grandfather's death had requested her presence at the reading of his will. After thinking it over, she had decided to come. After all, this would be her only opportunity to pay her last respects. After this day, she didn't plan to return to south Louisiana ever again. There was nothing here for her now. There never had been.

And on that thought, Brie bowed her head in final reverence to a man who had lived his life on his own terms regardless of the consequences. But unfortunately for her,

her broken heart would always be a painful reminder of the choices he'd made.

Drew Naquin watched her from a safe distance, knowing his presence at her grandfather's grave right then would have been an intrusion. After all, she deserved these few private moments alone with her memories of old Duke. He had been her grandfather, for heaven's sake. Perhaps in the eyes of the world not a very good one, considering the way he'd been and all, and Drew found it to be somewhat ironic that Brianna Stansbury was now the only living proof that Duke Bernard had ever existed at all.

Surprisingly, she hadn't changed much in all the years since he'd last seen her. Brie was still the spitting image of the woman Duke had married over fifty years ago and then deserted soon after, when the spark of adventure had taken root in his soul. And from what Drew knew of his old friend and colleague, Duke Bernard had never once looked back with regret.

Which was a damned good philosophy to live by, Drew reminded himself. In fact, he had adopted it as his own years ago. Even before he and old Duke had become friends. Because if there was one thing Drew had learned early in life about himself—mostly from being raised in the state's foster care program—it was that he was a survivor.

But unfortunately for Duke's granddaughter, she wasn't. Even from a distance, Drew could easily tell that much about her. She looked too thin . . . too pale . . . too vulnerable . . . too much in need of someone to hold her.

And if that wasn't enough to rip out his guts, God help him, she still looked too much like the young girl he'd intentionally hurt all those years ago. But he'd had no choice back then, any more than he would have had today.

Snapping the small twig he'd aimlessly picked up from the ground a few moments ago, Drew spun around and headed for his truck. After all this time, it was pointless for him to tell her that he was sorry for the way he'd handled things that night. Pointless and unnecessary. She'd probably forgotten all about it. And now that he'd seen her again and was certain that she wasn't permanently scarred by his callousness, he would, too.

And it didn't matter that he'd made a bedside promise to Duke as the old man lay dying. Dammit, he planned to keep his promise to his friend. He *would* look after Brianna…but he would do it in his own way. In much the fashion as Duke had, from a distance—from a very *distant* distance.

He had his own motives for doing it that way. Motives that really had nothing to do with Duke and the old man's reasons for wanting to keep his granddaughter at bay. *His* motives had more depth. They were deep down inside— rooted in his soul—and were troublesome, scary even, and Drew damned sure wasn't in any kind of mood to deal with them right now. In fact, if he was going to keep his lifestyle of seeking one adventure after another—which he most certainly intended on doing—then he never would.

Wanting one more glimpse of her before leaving the cemetery, Drew tossed a final glance over his shoulder before climbing into his truck and driving away. He chose to ignore the sadness that suddenly sneaked up on him and almost made him sick to his stomach with regret—the one emotion he'd practically guaranteed himself that he would live without. Dammit, how had he let that happen?

And even though it was Brianna Stansbury's God-given right to be here, he knew it would have been better for him if she hadn't come to Louisiana at all.

*   *   *

Taking a deep, calming breath, Brie smoothed out the knee-length narrow skirt to her pink tailored suit. Straightening her shoulders and with a deliberate briskness that belied her inner turmoil, she strutted into the office of her grandfather's attorney, Samuel Jacobs.

"I hope I'm not late," she said.

Immediately Jacobs rose to his feet and started around the left side of his large wooden desk to greet her. "No. Not at all. Come in, Miss Stansbury."

Hearing movement, Brie glanced to her right and watched as Drew Naquin slowly untangled his long athletic form from a sitting position. He looked good—*as tempting to her hungry eyes as ever.* But she had warned herself against the probability of his being here today and had taken extra precautions. Her emotional guards were more than just in place. They were armed and ready for battle. Still, it was quite obvious from the way her traitorous heart was pounding at the mere sight of him that she hadn't even tipped the scales when it had come to doing a good job of it.

"Actually, Brianna, according to my clock, you're five minutes late," Drew drawled in that lazy way of his.

Her eyes shot to his face and she wasn't surprised to find his expression serious and unwavering. Brie quickly recalled that it was that profound, complex look that had first attracted her to him. But, Lord knew, she'd learned the hard way that Drew Naquin's sober attitude was just an outer covering for what was really going on inside him. Beneath his skin, he was just as frivolous and carefree about life as her grandfather had been. "I'm sorry," she apologized stiffly. "I overslept."

Samuel Jacobs cleared his throat. "Uh…that's quite all right, Miss Stansbury. I'm sure the trip yesterday afternoon from Atlanta was long and tiring for you." Brie saw when he tossed a speculative glance in Drew's direction. Then, turning his attention back to her, the attorney smiled. "The reading of your grandfather's will shouldn't take very long, my dear."

"I hope not," Brie replied, taking a step forward while keeping a tight rein on her emotions. No one in the room needed to know how tough this was for her, she reminded herself, automatically glancing in Drew's direction. Least of all, him. "I've scheduled a late-afternoon flight home," she said.

Drew Naquin tossed her a glance, which she could easily read as one of pure relief. "Will you need a lift to the airport?" he asked.

"No, that won't be necessary," Brie said, dropping her eyes away from his. She had expected to feel a lot of things when facing Drew Naquin for the first time in nine long years, but not this sudden feeling of self-doubt. She'd come too far in valuing her own self-worth to allow that to happen. "I've made other arrangements," she said. "But thank you just the same."

Drew shrugged his broad shoulders. "Just thought I'd offer my services."

"Won't you have a seat, Miss Stansbury?" the attorney asked.

"Thank you," she replied, desperately hoping she didn't look as stressed-out as she felt. If the truth were known, she was beginning to realize that her coming to Lafayette was a mistake, and she wished she hadn't bothered at all.

Brie sat in the burgundy leather chair that was placed in front of the attorney's desk. Drew Naquin sat down right next to her in the one he'd occupied earlier.

"Anyone for coffee before we get started?" Jacobs asked.

Drew shook his head. "None for me."

Brie did the same. "Thank you, but I don't care for any."

"I thought you drank coffee," Drew said, giving her a questioning glance.

Brie slowly turned her head in his direction. "Well, I do," she responded in astonishment. The fact that he knew anything about her was surprising. "I've just had enough for now."

Drew simply nodded in response.

But Brie wasn't willing to let the subject drop there. "How do you know I drink coffee?" she asked, her expression guarded.

Drew shrugged coolly. "I've got a good memory for detail. I must have remembered it from that time I went with Duke to visit you. I guess it stuck with me because most kids that age wouldn't drink the stuff."

His reference to her as a kid dug deep into Brie's composure, but she forbade herself to show any reaction. Maybe she *had* been a silly teenager back then, but she'd had feelings all the same. Feelings he'd trampled on but good—without even a second thought. "Well, a good memory like yours must come in handy in your line of work," Brie stated.

He gazed at her then, a hard and unrelenting stare. "What is that supposed to mean?"

"Having to memorize the details of a treasure map. I would think that would require a good memory," she said. And although it hadn't been her intention to sound bitter, her voice had a biting quality to it.

"Look," he said, his relaxed posture becoming stiff, "I'm sorry you didn't find out about your grandfather's illness sooner. But that was the way he wanted it."

Now *that* hurt. Big time.

Tears would have started to fall, if Brie's resolve had been any weaker. But thank goodness it wasn't. Pity was the last thing she wanted from anyone—but especially not from Drew Naquin.

Lowering her gaze to her hands, which were now folded in her lap, Brie gave a slight smirk. "I'm not surprised," she said. Then she lifted her head, possibly a degree higher than necessary, and stared straight ahead. "So if you were worried that it would come as a shock to me to learn that my grandfather went to his grave not wanting me around, then stop worrying. I grew up a long time ago."

"I wasn't worried," he replied. "Just hoping you understood."

"Oh, believe me, I understood, all right. Considering the way my grandfather kept his world separate from mine, it wasn't hard for me to figure out."

Brie took a deep, calming breath and kept her eyes glued forward. But no matter how hard she tried to prevent certain emotions from springing forth, she found they did. One in particular—the one she knew was envy—really had a way of working her up. But it was something that she couldn't help. As far as she knew, Drew Naquin was the only person her grandfather had ever cared about. And, obviously, the only person he'd ever confided in. He'd treated Drew like a son, while he'd treated her as unimportant. The cutting blow was knowing that, even as he'd lain dying, it had been Drew—not her—her grandfather had wanted at his bedside. She envied Drew for having received from her grandfather what she had wanted so badly for herself.

And yet, knowing she was still that vulnerable inside upset her, made her angry with herself. Especially when she thought of all the childish capers she'd attempted over the years, hoping to win her grandfather's undivided at-

tention. There had been the time when she was ten and had
decided to throw him a surprise birthday party after he'd
telephoned to say he'd be in Atlanta on that date and
promised to come by to see her. Without her grandmother's knowledge, she had ordered a huge birthday cake in
his honor—complete with balloons and party favors for
everyone she'd invited—which had turned out to be almost all of the fifth grade class at her school. The total bill
for the extravagant birthday party she'd given him in the
hopes of winning over his love had ended up costing her
unsuspecting grandmother one hundred and twenty-five
dollars. But the worst of it was that her grandfather never
showed up on that day—nor did he bother to call and explain his absence.

Brie jarred herself from the painful memory and then
told herself that her presence here wasn't really needed,
certainly it wasn't necessary. Which was just fine with her.
She could have cared less.

So why didn't she just get up and leave?

Because she simply couldn't that was why. For one
thing, now that she'd come this far, if she left before the
reading of the will, Drew Naquin might somehow think it
was because of him. He might even think it was because
she still had that silly, stupid crush on him. And dear God,
that was the last thing she wanted him to think.

Her grandfather's attorney, who was impeccably at-
tired in a light blue three-piece suit, took a step toward her.
Brie could tell by looking at his perfectly groomed hair-
style that every strand of his graying hair was lacquered
into place. "Is there anything else I can get for you before
we start the reading, Miss Stansbury?" he said, smiling at
her.

"No, thank you," she replied, glancing in Drew's direction and noting that, unlike the attorney, the younger

man was obviously no slave to fashion. Drew's blue jeans were unapologetically faded and almost worn to threads in certain strategic areas—areas which Brie knew she shouldn't have taken notice of. To her, his light blue T-shirt was too tight for the occasion—after all, they *were* in a business meeting—though its snug fit certainly did command attention. Her attention that was. Enough so that Brie felt the inside of her mouth go dry. His red-brown loafers were scuffed and the light brown leather hat he had cocked back on his head looked as if it had taken a profound pounding of some kind. Still, much to Brie's regret, she had to admit that its fedora-like shape did give him a certain rakish, almost devil-may-care appeal. An appeal that she had tried to deny over the years.

And yet, even with all of that sex appeal oozing from him, she was in control of herself. That, in itself, was quite an accomplishment. If this had been nine years ago, she would probably have swooned at his feet. Today, however, she was sitting upright, with her chin held high. And she planned on keeping it that way, no matter how tough things got.

After looking at his wristwatch and sighing, Drew cleared his throat loudly. "Sam, let's get this reading over with, shall we?"

"Of course," Jacobs said, quickly returning to the high-backed black leather chair behind his desk. "We can begin now, if the two of you are ready."

"Well, I'm sure as hell ready," Drew replied.

"I'm ready, too," Brie replied, folding her hands in her lap and waiting for the attorney to begin.

Clearing his throat, Jacobs began the formalities of Duke Bernard's last will and testament. Before long, Brie was being told that her grandfather had bequeathed to her his old family homestead. And like the traitor she always knew her heart to be, it jumped ahead three beats at the unexpected news. She'd told herself she didn't want anything from him, and really, she didn't. Her sole purpose in coming to south Louisiana had been in the hope that it might help heal the wounds of the past. But then, inheriting her grandfather's homestead wasn't just anything. It was her grandfather's past, his ancestral history, and hers, as well. It was all she would ever have of him . . . of her roots . . . a lasting memory that he'd cared enough to pass on to her . . .

She wanted that house. According to the brief description that Samuel Jacobs was giving her, it was in a shambles now, but that was all right. Because one day—when she had the means—she would restore it to its natural beauty. But for now, just knowing that her grandfather had wanted her and no one else—not even Drew—to have the house gave her a warm feeling inside.

Looking over the rim of his glasses, Jacobs cleared his throat. "Are you all right, Miss Stansbury?"

Dabbing at the moisture that had collected in the corners of her eyes, Brie looked up quickly. "Yes—yes, I'm fine."

"Shall I continue now?"

Brie didn't know why she felt the need to look at Drew before answering, but she did. He must have felt her glance because he immediately turned his own eyes in her direction. Only this time, instead of glaring at her, he did the strangest, most unexpected thing. He lifted one corner of his mouth in a lopsided grin. Dumbfounded, Brie blinked before jerking her eyes back to the attorney. "By all means, please continue," Brie said in a rush.

"First, Miss Stansbury, I want you to understand that the house is yours, no matter what," Jacobs began.

Brie nodded. "I understand."

The attorney smiled and then adjusted his glasses to a different position on his nose. "Good. Because at this point, your grandfather's will becomes a bit more complicated.

"You see," he continued, "your grandfather saw fit to will the two of you—" he glanced from Brie to Drew "—a single gift that is to be shared equally, jointly."

"Jointly?" Drew asked. "What does that mean?"

"Exactly what it implies," Jacobs replied. "Jointly—together—as one."

Confused, Brie tilted her head to one side. "As one what?"

"As in one union," Jacobs continued. "In other words, in order for either of you to receive this gift, you must first marry."

"What!" both Brie and Drew exclaimed together, both shooting forward in their seats. Shocked, their eyes met momentarily.

"You heard me correctly," Samuel Jacobs replied calmly. "And you have only seventy-two hours—three days—to do so. At that time, if the two of you aren't married, to each other, then I'm to destroy the gift. And no one will be given the opportunity to examine it first."

Drew's eyes narrowed and a smirk forged on his lips. "What is this all about, Samuel? Duke never mentioned any gift to me."

"I'm not surprised," Samuel answered.

"So what is this gift?"

Jacobs cleared his throat. "A map."

The air rushing from Drew's lungs made a *swishing* sound. He leaned back in his chair. "A map?"

"What kind of map?" Brie asked, suddenly coming out of her temporary daze. She'd told herself it would be a mistake coming here. And she was right. It was a big mistake. A map? Marry Drew? Was her grandfather insane, or simply vindictive? He knew how much his adventurous ways had hurt his family, how she felt about men who desired drifting more than they did a family. She couldn't believe that even *he* would do such a thing as to tie her to an adventurer by willing her a treasure map.

"It's a map, Miss Stansbury, that your grandfather claims leads to Old Gabe's treasure."

"Old Gabe's treasure?" she asked, stupefied.

"Yes, there's a local legend about a pirate named Gabe and his treasure. Supposedly, it was buried in these parts sometime during the late eighteenth century. No one knows for sure if it even exists," Samuel said.

For the first time since arriving in Louisiana, Brie felt like laughing, but only because she knew if she didn't laugh, she'd end up crying. Truly, this was the topping on the cake. "I don't want it," she stated. Clutching her purse in her hands, she rose to her full height. "Now, if the two of you will excuse me, I have a plane to catch later this afternoon. Mr. Jacobs, you know where to reach me, if need be."

Determined to leave as quickly as possible, Brie whirled to go but stopped short when she felt someone grab her arm.

"Brianna, wait..."

She glanced back at Drew, her gaze hooded. Her heart was now pumping again—double time.

Drew had risen from his chair and was standing directly behind her. "I was thinking that maybe we could... Well, I guess you have a lot to do before boarding your flight home to Atlanta, huh?"

Brie dropped her eyes to where his long fingers encircled her arm, though it felt more as if they were around her heart. "Yes...as a matter of fact, I do."

Gentling releasing her, he took a step back. "Well, it was nice seeing you again. That's all I really wanted to say. That—and the fact that you look great...all grown up and all."

Gathering the courage that desperately wanted to run and hide somewhere—anywhere—Brie lifted her chin. "I am grown up—and all."

"Yeah, I can see that. I hope the man in your life knows how lucky he is."

Brie's insides froze. The truth was, she'd broken it off with her fiancé only a couple of weeks ago after one of his former girlfriends had enlightened her to the fact that he was nothing more than a scam artist. As it turned out, Carl Winthrop, her so-called "fiancé" was really a prime-time gigolo who chose his victims carefully. He enjoyed preying on women like herself who were virtually alone in the world. His game was to win over their trust, and then, when the timing was right, take them for whatever amount of money he could, then disappear without a trace. Anyway, Carl's true character had turned out to be so despicable, that by the time Brie had learned all there was to know about him, any good and caring feelings she'd had for him had been flushed from her body. As far as Carl was concerned, she had no regrets, except for the fact that she still felt somewhat foolish for getting involved with him in the first place.

But she certainly wasn't going to say as much to Drew. Actually, if anything, she wanted him to think that she *was* still engaged—and to a man who worshiped the ground she walked on. Call it pride, if need be. But it was what she wanted him to believe. It was what she *needed* him to believe.

She looked up at Drew and their eyes locked. The corners of his mouth lifted in a slight smile and for just a fraction of a moment, Brie thought she sensed a sadness in him. But it was only for a moment. Before she could respond, he turned away from her, in the blink of an eye moving to stand at the window, gazing out at something that had stolen his attention. Once she'd hungered for that attention. But not anymore. Not now that she was all grown up. She'd had her fill of men like him who played at life.

Suddenly Brie realized she had to get away—from him, from everything. "Excuse me," she said, quickly rushing from the office.

Within seconds she had departed from the attorney's building and was inside the small economy car she'd rented on her arrival at the airport. If she'd lingered inside a moment longer, she would undoubtedly have burst into tears right there in front of everyone. And that would have been a mistake. Because if there was anything about herself that she wanted to keep hidden from the world, it was the part of her that still felt frightened at the idea that she was alone in the world. Unfortunately, it was the same part of her that was still naive enough to dream of finding a man who thought she was worth his time and trouble.

Sometimes, no matter how hard she tried, she was still such a little fool.

Drew stood in Jacobs's doorway and watched as Brie disappeared from view. Something inside him disappeared right along with her, but he told himself that he damned sure wasn't going to give it much thought. If anything, he wanted to believe that the hollow feeling in the pit of his stomach was from hunger, and nothing more.

Besides, Drew thought with a slow shake of his head, he had enough on his mind, as it was. First off, what in the world had gotten into his old friend to make him decide to write his will as he had? And, second, where was all the money that Duke was supposed to have left Brianna?

On those troublesome thoughts, Drew pivoted and reentered Samuel Jacobs's office. "Okay, Sam," he drawled, readjusting his hat low over his eyes, which glinted with stern determination. "Now that Brianna is gone, I'd like to know what the hell happened to the two hundred thousand dollars that Duke told me he'd willed to her."

Chapter Two

Shocked speechless, Jacobs gaped as he stared at the younger man. Finally, after what seemed like endless moments, he managed to shrug and say, "I have no idea what you're talking about."

"Duke sold all his property and auctioned off all the antiques he'd placed in a colleague's private museum. Some of them were quite valuable. Except for the old homestead, he liquidated everything into cash just weeks before he died. Supposedly, he willed that cash to Brianna."

"Look, Duke came in here less than two weeks before he died, and I wrote up his will according to his wishes. A few days later, he came back and gave me the sealed envelope containing the map. But he didn't say one word about any money."

"Well, I know for a fact that it exists—somewhere," Drew replied. "And the last time Duke mentioned anything about it to me was just a few days before he died. He said that he'd fixed it so that Brianna would get everything."

"Well, don't look to me for an answer," Jacobs said. "I don't have it. Maybe instead of willing it to his granddaughter, he decided to squander it."

"He wouldn't do that. Besides, he didn't have time. And he would have told me if he had."

"He didn't tell you about the map, did he? And by the way, what do you think that's all about?"

"I don't know," Drew snapped, angry with himself because he didn't. Or maybe he was just angry with himself because his eyes had been so hungry for the sight of Brie that he'd missed some clue along the way.

He walked to the window and stared out. "Duke was dying and he knew it," he said in a hollow voice. "I guess that could make any man a little crazy...make him do some really strange things."

Then, continuing to stare out the window, Drew sighed heavily. Duke's last days weren't something he cared to recall. He'd lost a friend. Actually...he'd lost a damned good friend. Maybe the only person he'd ever been really close to.

"Anyway," Drew finally continued, "toward the end, Duke seemed to want to make amends for some of his mistakes—not that he actually admitted anything like that to me. He just started doing some strange things. Like the time he made me swear—on the Bible, no less—to look after Brianna." Drew glanced back at Jacobs, his eyebrows furrowed together. "Can you imagine that? Duke with a Bible in his hands?" Then he turned around and gazed out the window once again. "But I don't know what he was thinking when he made out his will. Maybe it was his way of trying to see to it that I kept my promise—as if he knew I wouldn't, even after I'd promised to."

"Hmm," Jacobs said. "I just wonder if it worked for him."

Drew frowned. "If what worked?"

Jacobs smirked. "Well, it sounds to me like old Duke was trying to buy his way into heaven—guilt-free. I just wonder if it worked."

"Duke wasn't a man who lived with regrets. Nor was he stupid. He knew he couldn't rectify a lifetime of blunders in one easy transaction."

"Well, we'll never really know for sure just what he was thinking, now, will we?"

"Well, I do know one thing, Sam. I've got to find out what happened to that money—and fast. With any luck, before Brianna flies out of here this afternoon." He walked up to the attorney's desk, braced his hands on the top and leaned forward. "You know as well as I do that the money rightfully belongs to her. Every last cent of it."

Jacobs pulled off his spectacles. "I agree with you, Drew. But the question is, just what did Duke do with it? Could it be hidden in that old house of his?"

Drew lifted his hands from the desk and rose to his full height. "No, I don't think he would do that," he replied, frustrated that he couldn't figure out what had become of Brie's inheritance. He rubbed the back of his neck. Surely he'd forgotten some small detail, something that Duke had said or done, that would solve this mystery. "Too risky. The way he kept house, all that money could catch fire."

"Do you suppose Duke really believed there *was* an Old Gabe's treasure?" Jacobs asked. "Maybe he spent—"

"No way...Duke and I both gave up on Old Gabe's treasure a long time ago. We both realized it was nothing more than local folklore."

"But the map—"

"The map has to be a fake," Drew cut in, running agitated fingers through his hair. "I don't know what was in his head at the time, but Duke knew I would never fall for it. In fact—"

Suddenly Drew stopped speaking in midsentence, and his expression froze in place. It was as if he'd been startled by a sudden blast of Freon.

"What's wrong, Drew? You look like you've just seen a ghost," Jacobs exclaimed.

Drew shook his head, trying to clear the confusion. But the stubborn notion he'd gotten a moment ago simply wouldn't budge. "My God, Sam.... Do you know what I've just realized?"

"What?"

Still shaking his head, Drew's hands automatically went to his hips. *"Duke buried Brie's inheritance."*

"What?"

Feeling a sudden rush, Drew jerked off his hat and flung it down in a nearby chair. "He buried the money, by golly. Why that old coot..."

"How do you know?" Jacobs asked, his face growing flushed.

Convinced that his gut feeling was correct, Drew allowed himself to race forward with it. "Old Gabe's treasure... of course... I should have realized it the moment I heard..."

"What are you saying, Drew, that Duke dug up an old treasure and then buried his money in its place?"

Drew shook his head. "No, no. Don't you get it? Duke buried his own money and then made up a map so that it could be found. Brianna's inheritance *is* the treasure. I know it sounds crazy—but now I understand what he meant when he told me that, if it was the last thing he did, he would fix it so that Brianna would be the sole beneficiary to his money. He planned this whole thing—the money, the map, the marriage—everything.''

By now, adrenaline was pumping through every cell in Drew's body. He felt almost dizzy from it. ''You see,'' he began, then stopped, trying to figure out how to explain to the attorney what he knew had to have been his old friend's motive. It wasn't going to be easy. Everyone who'd known Duke was aware that he'd been quite capable of pulling some rather unique stunts, but this time . . . Drew found that even he was having a hard time believing the story he was about to tell.

''Right before Duke died,'' he finally continued, ''he found out that Brie's fiancé was a first-class sleaze who targeted young, naive women—women like her, to put it bluntly. Duke figured he knew what was going to happen when he died and Brianna inherited from him. This boyfriend of hers was going to somehow swindle it away from her before she even knew what was going on. So, with time quickly running out for him, my best guess is he tried to figure out a way to keep that from happening. And he did. He buried his money, made a map and then made out his will so that his granddaughter would be forced to marry someone else in order to get her inheritance.''

Jacobs cleared his throat. ''But you don't know for a fact that's what he's done. You're only guessing. You could be wrong, you know.''

Drew shook his head in disagreement. He didn't have ESP, but he had some strong gut feelings that were just as psychic. ''I'm not wrong, dammit. I know I'm not.''

''But why wouldn't he have just told Miss Stansbury the truth?''

''Look, Sam, for you to truly understand Duke's motive, you've got to take into consideration his and Brianna's estranged relationship. They hardly ever spoke. It had been years since the last time. He knew he was the least likeliest person she would listen to, especially if his advice contained any kind of criticism—which, of course, this did."

Jacobs lifted his eyebrows in concern. "Well, if you're right, then it looks to me like he didn't think twice about dumping the whole messy problem in your lap."

"Yeah—well, he didn't have much choice, now, did he?"

"What do you mean?" Jacobs asked.

"He ran out of time, Sam. Duke simply ran out of time." At this point, Drew grabbed his hat and plopped it down on his head.

"What are you going to do?" Jacobs asked.

Drew's eyes narrowed. "I don't know."

"Well, if you ask me," Jacobs said, "I think it was preposterous of Duke to assume you would keep a promise that would end up demanding so much from you."

Drew looked at Jacobs. "I don't suppose you'd be willing to let me have a look at that map right this minute—without any strings attached—so I could see if I'm correct or not? If the map looks new, then I can be fairly certain that it was Duke who drew it up."

"I'm sorry, Drew, but I can't do that. I have certain ethics to follow and—"

"I understand, Sam. I was just making my point."

"And that is?"

"I have ethics, too, like keeping a promise to an old friend. And, unless I've missed something, the only way for us—me—to know for sure if Old Gabe's treasure is really Brie's inheritance is to go after it."

"But you'll have to marry Miss Stansbury."

"I know that," Drew snapped, not quite ready to deal with that detail yet.

"So, what are you going to do? Go to her before she leaves this afternoon and tell her what you've just told me?"

"Not on your life. After all, there's always the chance that I'm wrong. Right now, Brianna doesn't know that she should have inherited somewhere in the vicinity of two hundred thousand dollars. What do you think she'd do if I told her?"

"Well, if I were in her shoes, I'd want to know what happened to my money."

"Exactly. And just who do you think she's going to blame if I say I don't know what her grandfather did with it?"

"You?"

"You betcha. She's going to think I stole it from her."

"But she probably couldn't prove anything," Jacobs offered as a form of consolation. "Where are the records?"

"I don't know. Undoubtedly they're somewhere. Nonetheless, I'm sure that it would be just a matter of time before Brie found out on her own about the money. When that happens, if I've just sat back and said nothing about it, I'll look guilty as sin, now, won't I?"

"Okay, then. So what are you going to do?"

Drew sighed heavily. "Well, for starters, I'm not going to give Miss Brianna Stansbury any more information than I absolutely feel is necessary."

Jacobs shook his head. "You know, Drew, you don't have to do any of this. Legally Duke's will doesn't state anything about any money. The subject could be dropped, the map burned, the case closed. No one could accuse you of anything."

"I can't do that. I made a promise to Duke and I honestly believe that he wrote his will the way he did with the certainty that I would follow through on that promise. And even if that isn't enough to influence my decision, there's always the other thing to consider."

"What other thing?" Jacobs asked.

"If I take care of things now, I won't have to worry about Brianna in the future. What I'm trying to say is, a temporary marriage to her right now is better than a lifetime of having to commit myself to looking after her welfare. After I find her inheritance, she's on her own to live happily ever after—and if she doesn't then it's her problem, not mine. I'll be free of any obligation to her. And that, Sam, my friend," Drew added with emphasis, "is more reason for me to find her inheritance. I want my promise to Duke fulfilled and Brianna Stansbury out of my hair."

Jacobs shook his head. "This has got to be the strangest story I've ever heard. But then again, now that I think about it, it's so much like something Duke would do. So tell me, how do you plan to convince Miss Stansbury to go along with the terms of her grandfather's will? I don't think she's going to be very cooperative without knowing the truth first."

Drew smirked. "I don't think she would be very cooperative even if she *did* know the truth. But let me handle her, you just take good care of that map for the next few days or so. I'll be coming back for it."

"You mean *we*."

Drew halted, already on his way out the door. He glanced over his shoulder, quirking an eyebrow.

"As in you and Miss Stansbury," the attorney clarified quickly.

"Uh . . . yes, of course," Drew replied.

"Well, the map is one thing you don't have to worry about," Jacobs continued. "It's locked up, safe and sound, in a vault at the bank."

As much as he hated to admit it, Drew was almost disappointed to hear the map was under such die-hard protection. That meant there was no chance of his getting his hands on it without having to marry Brie first. Which was probably for the best, he knew, even if at some point—for just one fleeting second—he'd considered the idea of trying to steal it. But the only way to get it would be to blow up a bank, and there was no way he was going to do that. Too noisy.

He smiled at his own crazy idea. Under the circumstances though, who could blame him for having some crazy thoughts?

Jacobs cleared his throat. "Now, look here, Drew," he said, "whatever it is you decide to do, it has to be on the up-and-up. I'll have no part of anything illegal. I have my reputation to consider."

Drew turned to face the attorney. "Don't worry. I wouldn't get you involved in anything like that."

Jacobs glanced at his wristwatch. "Well, in that case, you haven't any time to waste. I have a feeling you're going to need every minute of the next seventy-two hours."

"Yeah, you're right," Drew said, picking up his hat from where he'd tossed it on the chair and adjusting it on his head once more. Frowning, he said goodbye to Jacobs and left the office.

But by the time he'd reached his pickup truck, he was surprised to find an unexpected excitement building in his gut. The kind of excitement he often got before starting a new adventure.

Well, he was about to embark on a new adventure, all right. And normally there was nothing Drew Naquin liked better than another new venture, another new gamble. Just the thought of it could stimulate his blood.

Only this time there was a catch. This time he had more at stake than ever before, and he needed to make sure that when it was his turn to sweeten the pot, he didn't ante up his heart by accident.

No matter how much he might be tempted to do so.

In a hurry to be on her way, Brianna packed hastily, tossing dirty clothing and fresh clothing alike into her suitcase without even folding each item. She wanted nothing more at the moment than to be gone. Gone. Gone. *Gone.* And even if she'd been offered a million dollars, she didn't think she could have made her wishes any plainer than that.

She'd removed her pink suit the moment she'd entered her motel room and now wore a pair of jeans and a red print shirt. She'd bought them just last week on her lunch hour from her job as an underwriter in one of Atlanta's most prestigious insurance firms. A red bandanna held back her shoulder-length hair at her nape.

Venting her anger on her wardrobe as she hurried around the room, she gathered her things, thoughtlessly slamming shut a dresser drawer on the end of one finger. The sharp pain punctured a hole in her resolve, and she was suddenly overcome by tears. Then the injury began to throb—and so did the sides of her head.

"Damn him," she exclaimed, angry with herself that, after all these years, after all the disappointments he'd caused in her life, she would allow her grandfather to continue to hurt her even after his death.

She wiped at the moisture on her face with the back of her hand. Discovering a box of tissues on the counter in the bathroom, she plucked one and blew her nose. All she needed to do right now was to keep one thing in mind. The sooner she finished packing, the sooner she could leave for the airport. And the sooner she did that, the sooner she would be able to put aside all the pain she'd found here.

And she'd though breaking off her engagement to her fiancé had been an ordeal. But that was nothing, compared to this.

Men. Her fiancé, her grandfather, the father she'd never known—and even Drew Naquin. They were all alike. Every single one of them thought first of themselves. Oh, they might have been willing to toss her a crumb or two of affection every now and then, but it wasn't something she could ever count on. And it was certainly not enough to fill the emptiness inside her.

Her stomach, now queasy, almost acidic from being empty for too long, made a gurgling sound. It reminded her that she hadn't eaten since yesterday. With the way her luck was going these days, she would probably develop an ulcer. Deciding it was best to eat something before boarding her flight to Atlanta later on this afternoon, Brie shut her suitcase, grabbed her purse from the chair and went out the door in search of a fundamental necessity for human survival—nourishment.

After making sure her room was locked, she headed outside. At some point during her stay, she'd noticed a small café down the street from the motel that advertised its hamburger platter as the best in town. She was more than willing to take their word for it and, starved, she started in that direction.

Hurrying along, she walked down one block and then rushed across the street to the next block right before the red light on the corner could turn green for the waiting cars. But just as she stepped up on the curb, a horn blew behind her, making her jerk around in surprise.

Immediately recognizing Drew Naquin as the driver of the red pickup with the loud horn, a surge of relief washed over her. She released the breath she'd held tight in her lungs. But while doing so, another emotion—this one having a bit more fire to it—began to seep through her body, causing her temper to rise. "You scared me half to death," she exclaimed.

His window was rolled down and his left arm was resting across it. He grinned. "Sorry. It wasn't my intention to frighten you, only to get your attention."

"Well, you most certainly did that," she retorted, trying her best not to let her temper—or any other emotion—get the better of her. It was just that seeing him again with that smile, when she hadn't expected to ever see him again, and knowing that he'd broken her heart once and she'd never completely recovered from it, rattled her to the core. And besides that, he *had* scared her. "What do you want?" Brie heard herself asking in a brisk tone of voice.

He shrugged. "Nothing too important. I just saw you strolling along, so I thought I'd stop you."

"Why?"

"I don't know why. Do I have to have a reason? I saw you walking down the street, that's why."

"Most people I know have a reason for what they do."

"Well, I'm not like most people you know."

"I won't argue that point."

"Where're you going?"

Wondering what was *really* on his mind, Brie studied his face for a clue. "To get something to eat before I leave for the airport."

"That's funny. That's exactly where I was heading, too. Care to join me?"

Brie continued probing his features. God, if he only knew how far she would once have gone—or how much of herself she would have once given—to join him anywhere in the world. But, thank goodness, she was past that point.

Liar.

"I don't have much time to spare," Brie said. "I'm just going for a hamburger."

Drew pointed down the road. "On the next block is Aunt Ada's. She has the best burgers in town."

"So I've heard." Brie began to walk in that direction.

"The barbecue double cheeseburger is the best."

"Thanks for the advice," she said over her shoulder, hurrying off ahead of him. But then she heard the wheels of his truck rolling forward and soon he'd caught up with her.

"Mind if I join you?"

Sighing, Brie stopped and looked at him. In the sunlight she could see that his dark brown hair had a few streaks of gray and the laugh lines at the corners of his brown eyes had deepened over the years. But his mouth was still wide and generous—kissable, she thought—and his teeth were still sparkling white against his sun-kissed complexion. At thirty-three, he was sexier than ever.

"Look," Brie said stiffly, "if this has anything to do with my grandfather's will—"

"I guess I can't fool you for a minute, now, can I?"

Not this time. Not if she could help it, he wouldn't.

She gave him a small smile. "Maybe for just a second or two."

That smile was back on his face. "That's it? Only a second or two?" Then, just as quickly, he became serious. "Look, I wouldn't have bothered you if it wasn't vitally important. If you'll just give me a few minutes to explain…"

Thoughtful, Brie stared off in the distance as a gentle breeze swept across her face. She heard a dog bark, a baby cry. Then she noticed the sun slipping out from behind a big white, fluffy cloud and brightening the earth again. No matter what, life moved on, renewing itself over and over again. Her only chance to ever find happiness was to go along with it. To endure. To try again. To never give up.

"We could call a temporary truce, couldn't we?" he asked.

Brie glanced at him swiftly. "Just what is it that you want from me, Drew? It can't be my grandfather's house. Jacobs says it's in terrible shape."

He shook his head. "It has nothing to do with the old homestead. At least, not directly." Motioning with his head toward the café down the street, he said, "I'll meet you inside."

Brie arrived at the diner before Drew, so she waited for him near the entrance. They decided on a booth near the jukebox and sat down. Drew motioned a plump, gray-haired waitress behind a low counter to bring over coffee. She filled two mugs, strolled to where they sat and plopped them down. "Okay, folks, what else can I get for you to-day?" she asked, a pad and pencil already in her hands.

Brie looked at Drew and shrugged. "A hamburger."

He looked up at the waitress. "Make that two barbecue double cheeseburgers—fully dressed—with fries. And two draft root beers."

The waitress was walking away as Brie took her first sip of coffee. "I should have ordered decaf," she said a moment later. "My heart's already pounding like crazy."

"Let me see," Drew said. Surprising her, he reached across the booth and placed his hand over her heart. His gaze bored into hers.

That was when her heart went completely bonkers, hammering against her breastbone as if it were going to burst through her chest at any second.

She inhaled deeply.

One way or the other, she was going to survive this day, even if it was the very last thing she ever did.

Endure. That was the key word.

But her brief lecture didn't stop her emotions from running through her body like wild horses turned loose in a canyon. In truth, her emotions had been running at that speed for a week now. Maybe this time she was going into shock.

Withdrawing his hand and allowing his eyes to soften their penetration of hers, Drew sat back and lifted his coffee cup to his lips. Finding the necessary strength to look away, Brie breathed a sigh of relief and took another sip of her coffee, reminding herself that caffeine was a stimulant and so, perhaps, a cure for shock.

She glanced at Drew and found him watching her through guarded eyes. She cleared her throat. "Found any buried treasure lately?" she asked, simply because she couldn't think of anything else to say.

One corner of his mouth lifted in a smile. He stirred a teaspoon of sugar into his coffee and then gazed up at her. "Not lately."

"Why not?"

He shrugged. "Too busy with other things, I guess."

"Oh... then you really must be feeling the itch for adventure."

"Yeah, sort of."

Brie forced a smile before saying, "So what's stopping you besides 'other things'? A girlfriend, maybe?"

"Not exactly."

Brie laughed. "What does that mean?"

"Well, it has to do with a woman, all right. But I don't think she classifies herself as a friend of mine."

"Oh? Why not?" Brie asked.

Drew shrugged. "I haven't the slightest idea. I happen to think I'm a fairly nice guy."

Brie laughed again in spite of the fact that their topic of conversation wasn't in the least bit amusing to her. He had a way of saying things that got to her. "Well, obviously, from what you've just said, she doesn't have the same opinion of you."

"Obviously not."

Brie felt a pressure building inside her. Who was this woman who had the ability to stop Drew from seeking his next adventure? she wondered. What kind of mythical powers did she possess? "Have you known her long?"

"Yes—and no."

Brie smiled slightly, but even that much was a pretense on her part. "Now what is *that* supposed to mean?"

"I've known her for years, but I've only been in her company a couple of times."

"Oh. Did my grandfather know her?"

Again, one corner of his mouth lifted in a grin. "Yeah, he knew her."

Now that rattled Brie but good, in spite of the fact that Drew was now grinning at her. Suddenly she had the strangest feeling, as if, maybe, he was talking about her. The thought was nearly paralyzing.

"Don't you get it, Brie? She's you."

"Me?" Her heart was pounding erratically.

"That's right."

"That's ridiculous. How would I be stopping you from going on your next adventure?"

"That's easy. I need your cooperation first, and I have a feeling you're not going to give it to me."

Brie sat back in the booth and took a moment to pull up all of her emotional guards. She would need them for this one. "Let me guess. You want your next adventure to be Old Gabe's treasure."

Drew didn't bother hesitating with his answer. "Exactly."

Brie smirked. "I guess I shouldn't be shocked, and yet, I am," she said, lifting her cup to her lips and praying that her hands weren't shaking as bad as her insides were. Because if they were, he'd know the truth about the brave front she was presenting to him. "I guess I should have known the temptation would be too great for you."

He remained sober. "Will you cooperate?"

Brie set her cup down on the tabletop without taking a sip. "Is that a coy way of asking me if I'll marry you, Mr. Naquin?"

Shoving his hat to the back of his head, Drew reclined against his seat and grinned. "Yeah, I guess so."

"Then allow me to make myself perfectly clear. My answer is no," Brie replied.

"Don't forget—you'll get half the treasure."

"Whatever that half would be, it isn't enough to make me marry you—or anyone." Brie leaned forward. "When—and if—I marry, it will be for love and nothing less."

"But this marriage would only be temporary. Just long enough for us to get the map and for me to find the treasure."

Well, of course it would be temporary, Brie told herself. Certainly she expected nothing more from him. After all, he was a temporary kind of guy. Here today, gone tomorrow. A woman would be a fool to think otherwise. "The answer is still no."

Shaking his head, Drew dropped his glance to the narrow tabletop separating them. "I knew you were going to make this difficult." Then he looked up at her with renewed determination. "I've got an idea. This time marry for money." Breaking into a grin, he placed his hand to his chest and said, "Hey, if I don't mind, then why should you? The next time you get married, do it for love, if that's what you think will make you happy. That's a simple enough request, isn't it?"

Brie felt her temper ignite. "You really have some nerve asking me to marry you so you can go after some silly buried treasure. Why don't you grow up, for heaven's sake? There are more important things in life than going traipsing around the world looking for adventure like some spoiled little boy."

He glared at her. "Grow up? Like you tried to do at age seventeen?" he growled.

His reference to that time in her life when she'd been so utterly foolish as to think the handsome young man who'd come to visit with her grandfather had an ounce of feeling almost shattered her composure. But somehow, she managed to hang on. "You *would* stoop so low as to remind me of the biggest mistake I ever made in my life. Well, now that you have, let me set the record straight. There were plenty of guys later on in my life who were more than willing to take me up on the same offer that you so *kindly* refused."

Drew had been sitting there, absorbing what he could of her, without actually losing control of himself. He knew that there had been nothing kind about the way he'd treated her that night. But at the time, he hadn't wanted there to be. She might just have been a kid back then, but her soft, innocent-looking eyes had said she wanted to become a woman—*his* woman. And maybe that was exactly why he'd reacted so harshly toward her. Maybe, in that one moment when she'd mustered the courage to approach him, he'd desperately wanted to make her his. But it would

have been wrong of him. Because afterward, he would
have left her, he would have had to. No, it wouldn't have
been fair of him to take her back then. Nor would it be fair
of him today. Because nothing about his way of life had
changed in the past nine years. He still thrived on adventure . . . on being free and in control of his life.

He always would.

Still, admitting that to himself didn't help his gut reaction to being told that some other guy—*guys*—had tasted
her sweet lips. In fact, it had come about a hairbreadth
from being more than he could take. Angry now, he
reached across the booth and grabbed her by the forearm.
"What in the hell did you do? Run all over the place like
some little fool, offering yourself to anyone and everyone
who happened along—just to ease your bruised feelings?"

"Yes," Brie said, forcefully, jutting out her chin. "And
now, if *I* wanted, I could probably teach you a thing or two
about life."

Drew knew she was lying. He could see it in the way her
eyes skidded from his. Dammit, she *had* to be lying. He
simply couldn't imagine her in such a role. He'd only said
what he had about her acting like a fool because he'd lost
it. And he felt certain that was how she'd responded to
him, too, in anger. Well, now that he was back in control,
he could play along with her little game for just as long as
she cared to. "Maybe I'll let you show me sometime.
Sounds to me like quite an adventure."

The waitress saved Brie from having to come up with an
answer to that one by appearing with their order and
plunking down the heavy restaurant-style plates in front of
them. "Can I get you anything else?" she asked.

"No," Drew replied, angry with himself for caring one
way or the other about the number of men Brie might have

had and angry with her for not telling him to simply mind his own business. It would certainly serve him right if she had.

The waitress sashayed off toward another table.

Drew knew he had to change his train of thought. Gathering up the big, juicy cheeseburger from the plate in front of him, he tried to concentrate on taking his first bite. Still, he heard himself saying, "You shouldn't talk that way about yourself, Brianna. Some people might actually believe you."

"And you don't?"

"I know better."

"You don't know anything about me. And neither did my grandfather. Of course, in his case, it was more by choice."

"Now, that's not entirely true. Duke did care about you—in his own way. You just never got the opportunity to see it."

"Well, I would have been more than willing to give him the chance to show me, but he never wanted it."

"Maybe he thought it was for the best if he didn't come around too often."

"Well, obviously it wasn't."

Brie felt her insides shaking and wondered if it were possible for her to crack into a million pieces. A million worthless pieces she was sure could never be glued back together— She grabbed her purse and jerked the long strap up to her shoulder with the intention of leaving. Sliding to the end of the seat, she said quickly, "Now, if you'll please excuse me, I must get on with my life. Undoubtedly you're in a hurry to get on with yours. Have a nice life, Drew." She rose.

"Now, wait just a minute," he said, immediately returning his burger to the plate and covering her hand with his other. "First of all, that is not why I brought you here. And second of all, would you please get that damned chip off your shoulder? I'm not the enemy."

She glared at him.

"Oh, all right, so you think I'm the enemy. It doesn't matter. Sit down. I need to talk to you."

Brie didn't budge.

"I said *sit down,*" Drew added with emphasis.

She sat stiffly on the end of the seat, not wanting to allow him to make a scene—she had a feeling he would do so with no hesitation whatsoever. She did not, however, slide her legs under the booth.

"Look, we have to go after Old Gabe's treasure."

Still piqued from his attitude, she turned her face toward him slowly. *"We?"*

"That's right. As in you and me."

"You might feel you have to. But not me," she replied, haughtily. "Obviously, I didn't inherit any of my grandfather's genes. I prefer to lead a normal, boring life."

"Well, obviously, you've inherited his stubbornness."

She glared at him and saw when the corners of his mouth lifted in a slight smile. Her heart skipped a beat. Damn him.

"Look, I need to go after that treasure and I can't do it without your help. You heard the terms of your grandfather's will."

"Let's get something straight," Brie said. "You don't *need* to go after that treasure. You *want* to go after it. There's a big difference."

"Okay," Drew said, now fully accepting the fact that he was going to have to come up with a damned good reason—a lie—in order to get her cooperation. Undoubtedly, because of her high sense of values, he knew it would have to be a darn good reason. One that threatened more than just a monetary loss to her, too. Something big, hazardous, would have to be at stake. He took a deep breath. "Either way, I don't see that I have much of a choice."

Brie stiffened her shoulders. "I don't know what that's supposed to mean. But, please, go right ahead. Explain it to me. I'm sure I'll understand. I'm a big girl now, remember?"

Drew gazed at her long and hard. "How can I forget, when you keep reminding me? But just who are you trying to convince, me—or yourself?"

Instead of answering, Brie dropped her eyes from his and took a sip of her now-cold coffee.

"Look," Drew began, not waiting for her full attention, "a couple of months ago, your grandfather got involved in a shady deal with some guys who weren't exactly model citizens—if you know what I mean. But I guess he figured he had nothing to lose. Anyway, something went wrong and he ended up owing them a lot of dough. And in order to get himself out of that big jam, he got himself into another. He went to a loan shark for the money and promised to pay him back within six weeks."

Brie's eyes widened. "A loan shark? But—but aren't those guys crooks? Why didn't you stop him?"

"Because your grandfather had the bad habit of not telling me when he messed up until it was sometimes too late," he said irritably. "Obviously, this was one of those times. Anyway, this guy—this loan shark—loaned him a lot of money."

"How much money?" Brie asked.

"I don't know exactly. Somewhere around two hundred grand."

"You're kidding."

"No, I'm not. But it gets worse," Drew said, glancing quickly around the room, acting out his part of the scam for her benefit. "I thought Duke had already repaid the money, but I found out yesterday that he hadn't. This guy—this loan shark character—paid a visit to me and said that Duke had told him I'd be a backup for payment if something went wrong and he couldn't come up with the money. So now this guy wants me to pay up...or else."

Brie's eyes widened even more. "Or else what?"

"Or else he's going to rough me up pretty bad."

"Like...like..."

"Yeah, like in the movies."

"Oh, my God," Brie whispered, her face growing pale.

"And if I tell anybody—the police, or Jacobs—he's liable to snuff me out completely. This guy means business. He doesn't care about anything but getting his money back."

Brie could hardly breathe. Her heart was pounding. "So what can you do about it?"

"That's obvious. Pay back the money."

Brie felt almost disoriented with shock—or maybe it was fear. "How will you do that?"

"I told you. *I've got to go after Old Gabe's treasure.*"

Brie felt the air gush from her lungs. "That's it? That's your brilliant plan for survival? You'll go on some wild-goose chase after a treasure that's probably worthless—if it even exists at all?"

"You have a better idea?" Drew asked. He fought to keep the smile off his face. This was turning out to be fun.

"You can borrow the money."

"And on what do you suggest I borrow that kind of money? I don't have any collateral," Drew stated. Actually, he had plenty of collateral, but that wasn't something he could tell Brianna, he reminded himself. "Do you have any money to loan me?"

Brie's head drooped. "Not nearly enough. I—I have four years of IRAs and a small savings account at my credit union, but that's about it." Then suddenly her head popped up. "Maybe the loan shark would allow you to pay him back a little at a time. Give him your word. Sign a promissory note, or something."

Drew looked at her as if she'd lost her mind. "This guy isn't interested in installments, Brianna. He wants his money now—the total sum—in cash. Old Gabe's treasure is my only hope."

"This is insane," Brie whispered.

Drew reached across the table and covered her hand with his. "Brie, you've got to help me. You're the only one who can. I've got to come up with the money, and soon. Old Gabe's treasure is my only shot."

"But... but we'd have to get married..."

"Look, if you'll cooperate, once I have the map, you can consider yourself free to go on with your life."

Brie tilted her head to one side and gazed at him. "Drew, are you telling me the honest truth?"

"Of course. Why would I lie?"

"Maybe you want to go after the treasure, but you don't want to have to share it with me like the will states. And if that's the case..."

Drew allowed his expression to grow into a look of utter disdain. "My life is on the line and you think I'm telling you this just to swindle you out of some money we aren't even certain exists?"

Brie felt about two inches tall. He was right, for heaven's sake. Drew Naquin wasn't Carl. Drew was an adventurer, not a gigolo. Not only that, but in a way, this whole thing was her responsibility. After all, it was *her* grandfather who had gotten him unwillingly involved in this mess.

How could she not agree to help him? If the situation had been reversed, wouldn't Drew have done the same for her?

The truth was, she had her doubts.

But that was beside the point. She was the kind of person who couldn't just turn her back on anyone. Not even Drew. She'd never be able to live with herself if she did. Especially if something happened to him as a result.

"Then I guess I have no choice, either. I—I'll help you," she said haltingly.

Immediately, Drew looked relieved. "Great." Then he looked down at his dinner plate. "As soon as we finish eating, we'll go to the courthouse to get a marriage license."

Brie pushed her plate to one side. "I'm not hungry anymore," she said. "How can you be?"

Drew glanced up, saw the questioning look on her face and added, "Hey, this could be my last meal."

"Oh, my God," Brie replied. Stricken with the reality of what was happening, she darted her eyes around the room, looking for what—or whom—she wasn't sure.

And Drew ate his cheeseburger in silence, all the while thinking about how much she was going to hate him when he finally told her the truth.

Then, again, he reminded himself, maybe it was for the best if she did come to hate him.

Either way, he disliked himself enough right then for the both of them.

It seemed loyalty to a friend came at a high price these days.

Chapter Three

It took Brie all of five minutes to make up her mind what she planned to do. But once she did, she decided to inform Drew immediately. "I'm going with you on the treasure hunt."

"No, you're not."

"Yes, I am," she said defiantly.

Drew frowned. "There's no need for that. In fact, it could be dangerous for you."

"Oh? And not for you?"

"That's different."

"It's not."

"Look," Drew said, leaning forward, "none of this mess is your fault. So just do what you have to do to meet the terms of the will and then let me handle the rest."

Brie stiffened. "And according to you, that is...?"

"Marry me so I can get the map and then go home to Atlanta. I'll be in touch as soon as I find the treasure."

"*If* you find the treasure," she corrected.

"I will find a treasure. Trust me."

"Well, I can't just go home."

Drew pushed his empty plate away from him. "And why not?"

Unfortunately for Brie, she didn't know exactly how to answer him. The truth was, she wasn't sure where her home was anymore. Atlanta seemed light-years away from what was happening in her life at this moment. "Look, I'm involved here—period," Brie stated. "My grandfather saw to that in the way he wrote his will. That alone qualifies me to go along with you. And besides, you might need my help," Brie added haughtily.

A look of disbelief crossed Drew's face. "I don't need your help in that way, and I don't want your coming with me. It's too dangerous."

"Well, now," Brie said, "that's too bad. Because I've already made up my mind to the contrary."

"Your attitude is just as bossy as his was," Drew said, rising from the booth. Crushing his napkin, he tossed it down on the tabletop and picked up the ticket the waitress had placed facedown near him.

Brie stood up, too. "I guess you're referring to my grandfather?"

Drew's eyes met hers, but he didn't say a word. After paying, he guided Brie from the café by placing his hand at the small of her back. But once outside, he began to argue his point again. "I'm telling you, Brianna, a hunt like this can be difficult—if not downright perilous. I won't let you come with me."

"Look, it's not just me I'm worried about," Brie said. "I don't want this guy hurting anyone—and that includes you."

He gaped at her. "And your coming along is going to solve that problem for me?"

"Maybe."

"Be real, Brianna. You're the type that probably has trouble swatting flies."

"Well . . . actually, I don't like swatting flies—but that doesn't make me incapable of helping someone in need."

"So, you think you're capable of fighting off the bad guys for me, right?" Drew asked sarcastically.

"Yes."

Though Drew was humored, he found his patience with Brie slowly losing ground. Why couldn't she be like him? he wondered, crediting his own resolve. He was hard-core. Tough. In fact, it seemed impossible that his simple promise to his dying friend could end up being such a problem for him. "Listen up," he said gruffly—possibly too gruffly, considering the shabby condition he sensed her emotions were in. "When the going gets tough in this old world, nobody gives a damn about you. It's every man for himself. So you'd better learn to take care of number one. Period. Got that?"

Brie stopped short and peered at him. "I can't think only of myself. What kind of a person thinks only of herself?"

"Well, you damned sure had *better* think only of yourself. 'Cause, babe, that's the number one rule of survival. Everything else pales in comparison. And by remembering that, you'll be doing us both a big favor," he added, his voice stern and unforgiving. "'Cause I won't always be there, watching out for you."

"I never asked you to look out for me," Brie said in surprise. "Personally, I think I do a fairly good job of taking care of myself, whether you believe that or not."

"Good—'cause that's how it's going to be between you and me. I don't plan to be anybody's caretaker for the rest of my life." He stormed off in the direction of his truck.

"Now let's get out of here. We've got to get a marriage license before the clerk of court office closes."

Frowning in his wake, Brie followed him. But for some reason, she stopped and glanced back. And when she realized that a stocky-looking man was quickly moving up on them, her chest squeezed tight with fear. *Oh, good heavens, the loan shark!* "Drew, there's a guy behind us."

"So?"

"He—he might be following us."

"Ignore him."

"But what if he's one of those...you know, loan sharks?"

"He's not."

"How do you know? You haven't even glanced back to see who he is," Brie whispered.

"Is he eight feet tall, with snow white hair and a gold tooth?"

"No," Brie stated breathlessly, not giving his odd description much thought. By now she was practically running to keep up with Drew's fast pace as she surreptitiously checked over her shoulder. "He's bald."

"Then it's not him."

"But—"

Suddenly Drew halted, causing Brie to come to a quick, stumbling stop. Within a matter of seconds, the man who had been walking behind them passed them by without mishap.

"See," Drew said meaningfully. "I told you it wasn't him."

"But how did you know?"

Drew caught her arm and began to lead her toward the parking spot where he'd left his truck. "Has anyone ever told you that you ask too many questions?"

"Maybe the problem is that I'm not getting any answers."

"You've been watching too much television."

"So I lead a boring life."

"That's your problem."

"I don't consider it a problem. Aren't you afraid?"

"Look, I've already told you. This guy wants his money. He's not going to come after me unless I fail to come up with the cash. Now, will you get that through your thick, stubborn head?"

Brie snapped to attention. "Yes, sir," she said, giving him a military salute. Piqued, she said, "Go ahead and get yourself killed—and see if I care." Which of course, she didn't mean and immediately regretted upon having said it. "I'm sorry," she blurted out.

"Don't worry about it," Drew said, marching them both toward his pickup. "I'm not going to get myself killed—not if I can help it," he added. Drew hadn't expected her to be so concerned for his welfare and he felt like a heel knowing he'd upset her for nothing. But he couldn't let himself worry about that now. He had a promise to keep.

After they were settled in his truck, Drew headed for the parish courthouse. Within minutes, he had them downtown, hunting for a parking space. They found one a block away.

The parish clerk working behind the counter in the department where they'd been directed met them with a smile. Drew asked her about obtaining a marriage license.

"You must wait a minimum of three days before the actual ceremony can be performed, but no more than thirty," the clerk replied.

"A minimum of three days? I wasn't aware of that. We can't wait that long," Drew exclaimed. "A lot of things can happen between now and then."

Like Brie could change her mind.

Like Brie could find out there isn't any loan shark.

It was simply too much time for her to sit—and think—and begin to question his story. "Is there any way of getting around this three-day waiting period?" Drew asked.

"Uh . . . well, yes. As a matter of fact, there is. You can get a judge or a justice of the peace to sign a waiver."

"Is that difficult to do?"

"I don't think so. They're fairly lenient."

"Good," Drew replied.

"Then I'll need your birth certificates and your social security numbers," the parish clerk replied, her smile renewing itself.

"I don't have my birth certificate with me," Brie said. "I'm from out of state."

"I see. Well then, do you have a driver's license?"

"Yes, I have that," Brie stated, rummaging through her shoulder bag to find her wallet.

Drew handed the clerk his duplicate birth certificate and his social security card. Glancing at Brie and seeing the odd expression that crossed her face when she realized he had the correct papers with him, he shrugged. "I just assumed that if we came this far, I would have to have proper ID."

"You must have been mighty convinced that I'd help you," Brie replied, a glimmer of suspicion snaking through her.

"Just hopeful," Drew said.

"Have either of you been married before?" the clerk asked without looking up from the document she was filling out.

"No," Drew replied. Then, with a cocky smile, he gazed over at Brie. "What do you think your fiancé is going to have to say about this?"

The young clerk raised her head. "Her fiancé…?" She pointed at Brie, but addressed her next question to Drew. "She has another fiancé?"

"Don't be ridiculous," Brie said, first forcing a smile in the woman's direction, then frowning in Drew's. "He just likes to joke around." A moment later the parish clerk was called away to answer the telephone. "How do you know about Carl?" Brie asked, narrowing her gaze.

After a moment of silence, Drew shrugged. "I don't know. I guess you mentioned him to me."

"No," Brie said. "I haven't mentioned him to you."

"Then I guess it was Jacobs."

Brie didn't recall mentioning her ex-fiancé to Jacobs, either. Then again, when the attorney had called to tell her about her grandfather's death, her life had been in such chaos due to the fact that she had just broken off her engagement to Carl earlier in the week. Her emotions had still been running high. Maybe she had mentioned her ex-fiancé's name. It certainly was possible, she supposed.

Either way, it was none of Drew's business what her engagement status was at this time. None whatsoever. If he thought Carl was still her fiancé, then so be it. "I'm sure he won't be very thrilled to hear I'm marrying someone else. Would you be if you were in his shoes?"

"If I were in his shoes, Brie, I wouldn't let you marry anybody else—not under any circumstances. You would be mine. Period."

Brie couldn't breathe. She could almost taste the pleasure of being his. "Oh," was all she could manage to say. Then, after regaining her emotional balance, she added,

"Well, I guess it's to your benefit that all men aren't quite as selfish as you are."

Drew gave her a quirky grin. "Well, under the circumstances, I'd have to say you're right. So when are you going to telephone him with the news, before or after the wedding takes place?" Drew asked, his eyes challenging her.

"Uh...actually, neither. I think it's best if I wait until I get back to Atlanta."

"I guess this is going to delay your original wedding plans, right?"

"Actually...no."

Drew's eyes penetrated into hers, hard and unrelenting. "Tell me, how much do you really know about this guy?"

"What kind of question is that?" Brie asked, avoiding his intense gaze. Boy, did he ever have some nerve.

"Are you in love with him?"

"That's none of your business," Brie said, her insides quivering. Certainly, if she'd ever loved Carl at all, it wasn't anywhere near the way she'd once felt about Drew. She could see that now. Still, it wasn't something she was going to admit out loud. Not to him. Not to anyone.

"Look," she continued briskly, "just because I'm marrying you doesn't give you the right to pry into my private life."

Drew's expression grew stiff. "I wasn't prying. I was simply asking a question. A logical question, I might add, for someone who's getting ready to marry the guy."

"That'll be twenty-five dollars," the parish clerk suddenly injected into their conversation, putting an end to their discussion.

Drew paid the amount with a check, thanked the clerk for her help and then hurried out, with Brie following right beside him.

"Now to find a judge or justice of the peace who's willing to sign the waiver," he said as they hustled across the street to the next block. His truck was parked just around the corner. "Maybe Samuel Jacobs can help us in that department."

Drew spotted a phone booth against the side of a building, and while Brie waited nearby, he telephoned Jacobs and asked the attorney if he knew of someone who would marry them as soon as possible. Jacobs agreed to call a judge whom he knew and told Drew to telephone back in an hour.

"We've got some time to kill," Drew said, after explaining the details of the phone call to Brie. "It's probably as good a time as any for us to shop for the supplies we'll be needing for the hunt—especially if you're still insisting on coming with me . . ."

Brie nodded. "I am."

"Then you're going to need some warm clothing for the outdoors. There's a small cold front dropping down from Canada. The local weathermen are predicting that it will reach here by late tonight."

Brie cocked her head to one side. "Can I ask you something?"

"Now what?" he replied, his stride never altering once as he continued forward.

"Do you ever work? I mean, do you hold down a regular job—get a paycheck like most folks do?"

He shrugged. "Depends on what you mean by work."

Brie gestured with her hands. "Work—as in nine to five—I think you know what I mean."

"Yeah, I work," Drew replied.

"Where?"

He grinned at her. "Look, just because you're marrying me doesn't give you the right to pry into my personal life," he said, happily reminding her of her earlier comment.

Brie glared at him in silence.

Having made his point, Drew's grin widened. "Hey, but look, I've got nothing to hide. Therefore, I'm going to answer your nosy question, anyway," he said teasingly. "I buy real estate—businesses, land, homes. I have the buildings and homes remodeled, then I rent them out. I buy land, then I rent it—or sometimes sell it—to farmers, developers—whoever's interested. Anyway, it's enough to pay for my life-style and then some. But more important, it affords me the time off I need to pursue my other interests."

"Like searching the world over for buried treasure."

He gave her a knowing look. "That's right. Among other hobbies."

"Sounds like a pretty carefree life-style, if you ask me."

"I don't answer to anyone but myself. So, yeah, I'd have to agree with you. It's a pretty carefree existence. But that's the way I happen to like it. I have everything I want."

"Except roots," Brie replied.

His eyes suddenly became guarded. "Like I said, I have everything I want. Anything more would only tie me down."

Brie smiled sadly. "And I'm just the opposite. I need to know I have roots somewhere," she replied.

Reaching his truck, Drew opened the passenger door for her. "I know," he said in a tight voice. He waited for her to climb up and settle inside the cab before shutting the door. Then he went around to the driver's side and got in. Both of them remained silent for the next several miles.

A few minutes later, Drew pulled in at a gasoline station, and after filling up the tank, checked the engine. Brie went to the rest room located around the side of the building and then walked inside to buy a pack of gum. Swinging open the wide, heavy door in order to exit, she froze in place when she saw a stocky man filling up his car at the gasoline pump opposite Drew. There was something familiar about him.

Then she realized that he looked very much like the same guy she had seen following behind them in town. Her stomach muscles tightened. *Maybe he was the same man and maybe Drew had been wrong about him. Maybe the guy was waiting for the perfect opportunity to jump his victim.* But then the man finished and turned in Brie's direction and she realized it wasn't the same person at all. Relieved, she released the oversupply of oxygen she'd held tight in her lungs. Then her eyes swung in Drew's direction and she thought about what his reaction would have been had she yelled out for him to run for safety—which, in all honesty, for a moment there she *had* been about to do. Good grief, but wouldn't he have been furious with her, if she had?

And she would have been so humiliated.

In front of him.

Again.

Actually, though, if the truth were known, it was Drew's attitude toward the danger that existed for him, not hers, that had *her* concerned. How could he be so careless...so easy and casual about what could happen to him? Was it his way of trying to deny the horrible reality of it? If that was the case, he'd created a false sense of security. One that could easily get him hurt—real bad.

And just the thought of what could happen to him terrified her.

Yet, Brie knew it was useless to voice her fears to Drew. She knew he would only start the same old lecture on the number one rule of survival. And she'd already heard that speech once today. Twice would definitely be too many.

By the time they arrived at the wilderness supply store located on the opposite end of town, an hour had passed. Upon entering the supply store, Drew immediately asked the salesclerk if he could use the telephone, and the woman handed it to him over the counter. Before long, he was speaking to Samuel Jacobs again.

"Why not?" Drew asked, furrowing his eyebrows as he waited for the attorney to answer him. After several seconds, his frown deepened. "Are you sure about this guy, Sam?" Then once again, he paused to listen. Finally, right before hanging up, he added, "All right, then. First thing in the morning."

"What is it?" Brie asked the moment the conversation ended.

"Jacobs's friend says he'll sign the waiver and marry us, but he can't do it tonight. He has plans. But he's willing to marry us in Jacobs's office at nine o'clock in the morning."

"So now what?"

"So now we wait until morning," Drew said, peeling off his leather hat and running frustrated fingers through his hair. "I guess we could always use the time tonight to get ourselves ready for the expedition."

"Yeah, I guess so," Brie replied, wondering if that meant they were going to be together for the entire night. If so, that translated into a whole lot of time—from now until morning. Just how much preparation needed to be done before going on a treasure hunt? As far as Brie knew, there were only two things necessary—a map and a shovel.

Drew had mentioned that the wilderness supply store would have just about everything they would need for the hunt, and after scanning the well-stocked aisles of merchandise, Brie had to agree with him. The front of the store was the clothing department. Then, starting about midway down and continuing as far back as Brie could see, the rest of the building was used as a supply headquarters for what she assumed were some of the area's more popular outdoor activities, like hunting, fishing, camping and boating. And if a person didn't happen to know how to participate in any one of these activities but wanted to learn about them, there were plenty of books in a special section of the store that could help one get started. While waiting for Drew to decide what he needed, Brie quickly thumbed through several, but she didn't see anything on treasure hunting.

"Can I help you, ma'am?"

Brie glanced over her shoulder and saw a pleasant-looking salesclerk who looked to be in her early twenties. "As a matter of fact, yes. I need a pair of hiking boots."

The saleswoman smiled. "The gentleman you came in with asked me to tell you to be sure to get everything you might need. He also said for you not to worry about the cost, he has an account here."

"Does he now?" Brie asked curtly.

The salesclerk nodded. "Actually, he's a very good customer here. So is his friend."

Brie's heart stopped. "His friend?" *Girlfriend?*

"Yes. An older man, tall, thin, gray hair."

Brie's heart started again. "Oh. That must have been my grandfather. He died a week ago."

"I'm terribly sorry," the clerk said, genuine sympathy in her voice. "He was such a nice man." Then the woman peered at Brie. "You know, now that I'm aware of it, I can see the resemblance in the two of you. Around the eyes, I think."

Brie smiled sadly. Actually, she'd always thought she had her grandmother's eyes—which only went to prove that people often saw what they wanted to see in others. In this case, the person was doing so out of kindness. "Thank you," Brie replied. Then she turned her attention to a rack of denim jeans that were marked down by twenty percent. She found her size, moving on to a group of shirts that were hanging on a display rack near the middle aisle.

A few minutes later, after scanning through dozens of colorful shirts and vests, Brie developed the intense feeling that someone was observing her every move. After several more seconds, she became certain of it. Knowing it wasn't the salesclerk—Brie could see her helping another customer—and thinking the absolute worst—as in, was it the loan shark?—she glanced around quickly and was surprised when she suddenly made eye contact with Drew. He was standing about ten feet behind her, one shoulder leaning against a rugged-looking support post, watching her through lazy, half-shuttered eyes. Eyes that had a way of torching her insides into a raging bonfire.

"What is it?" she asked him briskly, startled to find him there. "What do you want?"

He shook his head slowly. "Nothing."

"Then why are you staring at me?"

"Maybe I just like watching you when you're not aware of it."

"Why?"

Breaking into a lopsided smile, he shrugged. "I don't know. Maybe I'm just trying to figure out what makes you tick."

Brie felt as if she were ticking away, all right. Like a time bomb—ready to explode. "Well, don't bother," she said, waving her hand in a casual gesture that suggested she was feeling just the opposite. *Why in the world would he want to know what made her tick?* "Even I haven't been able to figure that one out yet."

"Ah...but don't you see? That's what makes it so much more of a challenge."

Brie tilted her head to one side. "Does everything have to be an adventure to you?"

Drew hooked his thumbs in his front pockets. "Actually, most things in life are, if you stop and think about it. Some things have to be helped along the way, but not many."

"And do you think I'm one of those *'things'* that have to be helped along the way?"

Drew pushed himself away from the wooden post and sauntered to her. Running his fingertip down the bridge of her nose, he said, "I don't know yet. That's part of what I'm trying to figure out." He leaned forward and kissed her hard on the mouth, shocking her speechless. Then, just as quickly, he pulled away. "And when I do, I'll be sure and let you know," he said, walking off into the men's department without saying another word.

Finally, when Brie was able, she simply added, "You do that." Then, still somewhat dazed, she walked into the dressing room with an armload of clothes to try on.

The salesclerk who had walked off to help another lady saw when her first customer, the pretty young woman with the red scarf in her hair, was suddenly and thoroughly kissed by the good-looking man who had accompanied her inside. And of all things, it had happened right there in the middle of the store, with everyone watching. So far, today had been just another uneventful workday for her and her colleagues. But things were definitely looking up.

Brie examined herself in the long mirror in her dressing room. Tomorrow morning she was getting married. Under normal circumstances she would have been wearing her dream wedding gown, a floor-length, long-sleeved white lace dress that accented her narrow waistline. She would have been getting married in a church, with flowers and candles and organ music. But normal hardly described what her wedding to Drew was going to be like.

Therefore, taking this into consideration she chose her wedding ensemble accordingly: a pair of chocolate brown denim jeans, a bleached indigo denim shirt, a blue-and-tan designer flannel vest with bone-colored socks and camel-colored hiking boots. In lieu of a veil, she chose a hat with the brim cocked up on one side. It matched her camel-colored boots to a tee.

Instead of a bouquet, she guessed she would carry a backpack.

Suddenly, though, as quickly as it had come, Brie's light mood vanished and she felt herself sinking low. She would really have to do some talking to keep herself on an even keel. She knew that she was getting all upset over nothing. So what if she was wearing jeans on her wedding day? Someday, hopefully in the very near future, she would have another wedding, a real wedding, and another chance to wear her dream dress. Someday soon, she would meet and fall in love with a nice guy who would love her back. And together they'd gladly make whatever personal sacrifices necessary to insure their love forever. Her dream-come-true was that she and her husband make roots for themselves, and for their children and their children's children. This had been her secret wish for years now. And she wasn't ever going to give up on it.

The salesclerk, who had been going back and forth to bring Brie additional clothes to try on, came into the dressing room and offered her the option of walking out beyond the dressing room area to show Drew the outfit she'd chosen. Brie found herself declining the invitation.

After all, this *was* her wedding attire, and tradition, as a whole, ruled against the groom seeing the bride in her dress before the actual wedding day. It was considered bad luck. Who knew, maybe the same held true for jeans and hiking boots. Regardless, she wasn't taking any chances. To bring bad luck down on them could mean they wouldn't find Old Gabe's treasure—or if they did, it would be worthless. Simply put, Drew needed all the good fortune he could get. And to be perfectly honest, she did, too.

After re-dressing in her own clothes, Brie gathered her intended purchases and went in search of Drew. She found him at the checkout counter, stacking his own selections near the cash register. As she walked up, he took the items that she held and dumped them next to his. "Did you find everything you needed?" he asked.

Brie ignored that question in lieu of saying something she thought more important. "I'll pay for my own purchases."

Choosing to ignore her, Drew pulled out a credit card and handed it to the clerk.

"Drew," Brie began, not wanting to make a scene but definitely unwilling to let him pay for her purchases, "this is not going to work." Her voice sounded firm and in control.

"So owe me," Drew replied. "Right now, we need to get out of here. I noticed a tall guy in the dressing room and a—"

"Oh—God! Where is he now?" Brie cut in. Suddenly she felt breathless—and guilty for not paying closer attention to what was happening around them. Like a scatterbrain, she'd let herself become so wrapped up in her new wardrobe, she'd forgotten her real purpose for being here with Drew.

Drew leaned toward her and whispered in her ear, "He was still in the dressing room when I came out."

Eyes wide now with caution, Brie quickly glanced back at the entrance door to the men's dressing room. "He followed you in there?"

"Uh-huh," Drew said as he accepted a ballpoint pen from the cashier and signed his name on the credit receipt. He smiled at the older woman as she handed him their packages. Then, taking Brie by the elbow and ushering her toward the door, he said, "Let's get out of here."

He didn't have to tell her twice. Nor did she ask any of her usual one hundred and one questions that might delay their parting. In fact, Brie scrambled out the door and was inside the truck in fifteen seconds flat.

But according to her—now that adrenaline was mainlining its way into her blood—Drew was too slow in getting the engine cranked for their getaway. And when they finally started moving, only to stop for a slow oncoming car going by, she angrily informed him that unless he got them going faster, the next time they needed to make a hasty retreat, *she* was going to be the one doing the driving.

In response, she heard him curse under his breath—first, at himself, and then at her grandfather—for the fine mess he found himself in. Then he glanced over at Brie. "You know the deal about the tall guy with snow white hair and a gold tooth?"

"Yes," she replied warily.

"Doesn't his description sound kind of extreme—like something from a 1960s spy novel?"

Pausing to consider his question, Brie frowned. "Uh . . . yeah—maybe so."

"Well," Drew said, drawing in a deep breath, "the truth is...back there in town when I asked you if the guy you saw fit that description—" her eyes widened as she waited for him to continue "—well...I was only making a joke."

It took all of a second for her expression to close. When it did, she turned away from him, sat erect and stared straight ahead in dead silence.

From the corner of his eyes, Drew glanced at her. "I thought you knew that from the start."

Seconds ticked by. Finally, she said stiffly, "Obviously, I didn't. How stupid of me. I guess I must have been too concerned for your welfare to give what you were actually saying about him any serious thought. But of course, that was before I truly understood the number one rule of survival. Surely, now that I know better—and have had time to think things through—I won't make another mistake like that again."

Suddenly realizing how upset she was and inexplicably warmed by her concern for him, Drew reached across the seat to touch her hand. "Hey, look, I'm sorry," he said.

Brie jerked her hand away. There was a saying about ignorance being bliss. Well, according to her, ignorance had a price. Am embarrassing price. "Well, then tell me," she said, her posture still rigid. "If he doesn't have snow white hair and a gold tooth, just what does this loan shark really look like? And this time I want the truth, Drew."

Chapter Four

He should have known she'd ask that question.

"Like nobody special," Drew replied gruffly, growing more and more frustrated with himself, with her, with the whole situation he found himself in. He'd been right in thinking that loyalty to a friend came at a high price. It came at a damned, frustratingly high price. "He just looks like an ordinary guy. No scars."

"No gold tooth," Brie injected, but the humor she'd intended failed her.

"No. Nothing to single him out in a crowd, okay?" Drew said, now taking his turn at staring silently ahead. Something—a crazy, disturbing feeling—hit rock bottom in his stomach.

He should have known something like this was going to happen to him. Hell, it had happened to him nine years ago. The first time he'd seen Brie, he'd known that there was a certain quality to her that made him feel different inside. Not that he'd encouraged or even nurtured the feeling. It had just stayed, no matter what he'd done to discourage it. And sometimes—more often than he cared to think—it came back to haunt him. It was a special kind of feeling, one that he couldn't quite put his finger on. But he knew when it was there. And sometimes—like now— that sensation made him wish that he were different. Or maybe it was simply a wish that *she* were somehow different in her expectations of him. But if Drew knew anything at all about this old world, it was that wishful thinking never changed a thing. Still, deep down inside, Drew knew that if he would have wanted to have loved someone, Brianna would have been the one. Hands down.

But of course, he would never allow himself to feel such a thing. Because if he did, he would lose too much of himself—his independence, his freedom—and already it had taken him all this time to get back what he'd lost of himself as a foster child. Uh-uh. No way. He might thrive on adventure, but not that kind.

He'd kissed her, dammit. Right there in the middle of the store.

He still could hardly believe he'd done it.

But he damned sure had. And though it had been a quick, impulsive act on his part, he could still taste her sweetness. A sweetness that she'd offered him once, a long time ago. And sometimes—practically every night since then—he regretted the way he'd handled her feelings. But at the time, he'd been shocked—and, yes, tempted—by her innocent offer. He had done the only thing he could. He'd simply turned and walked away.

Drew glanced over at Brie, inwardly shaking off his un-settling feelings. "Look, I'm telling you, you're worrying yourself sick over this guy for nothing."

Brie crossed her arms over her stomach. "Fine," she replied angrily. "I won't ever mention him again. After all, it's your life at stake, not mine."

"That's right," he replied. "He's my worry, not yours."

"Thank goodness."

"You're right about that."

Silence fell between them. Finally, in a cool voice, Brie asked, "Where are we going?"

"To your motel room."

Her indifferent attitude vanished. She stiffened. "What for?"

"Your things. I'm checking you out of the motel, and you're coming with me."

"Where to?"

Good question. Drew had been trying to determine that himself. From now until morning was too long a period of time for Brie to be alone—and think. So he'd had to come up with a better game plan. And now that he had, the more he thought about his idea, the more he liked it. Camping out on a cold night like tonight could put a whole new perspective on their situation. No telling what could happen when the temperature dropped and the windchill factor kicked in. By morning, Brie might very well have changed her mind about accompanying him on the treasure hunt. Lord knew his emotional state would be thankful for the break. Yep, the more he thought about it, the more he thought this idea of his could very well work to his advantage. "Let's just say that for now, it's a surprise," he replied, grinning at her.

She frowned in his direction. "I don't like surprises."

"Yes, you do."

"No, I don't."

"Well, I think you'll like this one."

"If we're not getting married until tomorrow morning, why can't I remain in my motel room tonight?" Brie asked.

"We need to stay together."

"We do?"

"Uh . . . we do. But not in a conspicuous place like your motel room," Drew replied, trying to quickly come up with a good alibi for what he had to say. It had to be something that would satisfy her.

Wasn't it strange how one simple little lie seemed to lead naturally into another?

He was getting himself in deeper and deeper. At what point would he stop—or rather, at what point *could* he stop?

He knew the answer to that. He couldn't stop until he'd fulfilled his promise to Duke. And for now, the only way he could justify his deceitfulness with Brie was to keep telling himself that he was doing it all for his old friend— and that she, after all, was the one who would benefit in the long run. "I think we ought to stay together some- place where no one would think to look for us." When Brie's eyes widened, he shrugged casually. "Just to be on the safe side."

"You mean hide out?" Brie asked anxiously.

"Not exactly. But, yeah—I guess it's kind of the same thing."

"So, you do think you're in danger," Brie stated.

"No, I don't think I'm in danger. I'm just playing it safe, that's all," Drew replied.

"Where will we go?" Brie asked.

"Your place."

"Atlanta?"

He laughed at her. "No, Brie. Duke's old place. It's yours now, remember?" When she didn't answer him, he continued. "I don't think anyone would come looking for us out there."

Brie's heart was pounding with excitement at the thought of going to her grandfather's home for the first time in her life. "You mean the house is open? We can just walk in?"

Drew looked over at her and gave a lopsided grin. "Brie, the place is yours. You can do whatever you want with it. But, the truth is, I have a key to the front door. Your grandfather gave it to me years ago."

The fact that he had a key to her property when she didn't, should have bothered her. But, for some reason, it didn't.

"You're right," she said, taking a deep breath and looking ahead. That grin of his only added to an excitement that already had her heart beating like crazy. "I guess the idea that it's mine now just hasn't sunk in yet."

"Look, I need to warn you. The place is—well, nobody's been in there in months. The electricity has been cut off, which means no lights, no heat. And like I said before, there's a cold front coming in. But we should be okay. I've got lanterns and there are a couple of fireplaces in the house—and an old cistern out back for water. We shouldn't need anything else. Not just for one night."

"Bathrooms?" Brie asked.

"*A* bathroom," Drew said, "that was added on after the original house was built. But I don't know what kind of condition it's in. In fact, your grandfather was staying with me when he died, so I haven't been inside the old house in a while."

Grandfather should have been staying with me, Brie thought to herself. I should have been the one trying to nurse him back to health.

But, thank goodness, her emotional guards were doing their jobs for now. She could deal with these kinds of thoughts without giving out a clue as to what she was feeling on the inside. "Is there any furniture?"

"Very little. Old Duke wasn't there much anymore, and besides, he never was very interested in furnishing the place. I'm sure everything inside is in pretty bad shape. Look . . . now that I think about it, maybe this isn't such a good idea, after all."

"No, please," Brie said quickly, placing her hand on his forearm. "I'd really like to go. I can handle whatever condition it's in." She looked at him earnestly. "Believe me, I can."

Drew's eyes dropped to where her hand covered his arm.

"I'm no sissy, Drew."

His eyes shot to hers. "So you keep saying. But this treasure hunt is different. I don't think you understand what you're getting yourself into. For starters, I feel almost certain that we'll be heading into the Atchafalaya Basin. Have you ever been in a swamp?"

Brie shook her head. "No."

"I didn't think so. You don't seem to realize that your inexperience will only cripple the expedition."

"Look," Brie said, feeling as though she were defending herself for the hundredth time, "I might not be as experienced as you, but I learn quickly. With a little patience—"

"There isn't enough time to teach you anything. Plus, I don't have that kind of patience. If you're that determined to come along, then you'd better be ready to keep up from the start. No one gets special treatment from me," he warned.

Brie gazed at him for a long moment before saying, "I haven't the slightest doubt that you mean every word you just said. Now, does that make you feel better?"

In response, he glared straight ahead.

After a moment, Brie shrugged off his intimidating silence and moved as far away as she could on the passenger side of the truck. Leaning her head back against the seat, she closed her eyes with the intention of resting for a moment or two. She never realized when she dozed off.

Drew saw when Brie fell asleep. Refusing to dwell on the fact that he suddenly, urgently, wanted her near him, he told himself that she was in danger because she was leaning against the unlocked passenger door. Assuring himself he was only coming to her rescue, he eased her over until her head rested against his shoulder.

By now he was driving through an area of town where several small retail shops lined the highway. One store in particular, a lingerie shop with a single window display, grabbed his attention. The two long-haired mannequins in the front window were wearing crisp white cotton lingerie that looked to be about as turn-of-the-century-conservative as any style could get. Their high necklines, tucked bodices and lace trimmings left plenty to the imagination. And boy, did Drew ever have an imagination. Especially, right then, with Brie snuggled up against him.

He could just picture her all decked out in a crisp white cotton gown, with dainty buttons closing up the high neckline. He could almost feel the sweet anticipation that would be sure to come as his fingers tugged at the many tiny buttons keeping her warm, tender body from his view, from his touch. And then...when finally the gown was opened and she was his at last...

Damn, he was getting hot just thinking about them together.

At that moment, the right tires on Drew's truck hit the shoulder of the road, jerking his attention back to the present. Cursing at his thoughtlessness, he veered his vehicle back onto the highway. Then, lowering his window, he poked his head outside and inhaled a lungful of cool night air. What he wanted more than anything right now was to switch his oversensitized brain to other matters. Matters of more importance. Like survival. *His* survival. Because imagining Brie—even in ultraconservative, turn-of-the-century old garments—made his heart race.

And to be perfectly honest, it scared the hell out of him to think that one person—one little female, mind you, whose slender build was no match for his massive strength—could have that much control over him.

He had to put a stop to this craziness right now.

Easier said than done, he soon realized, when images of Brie simply refused to disappear. So when he saw a sign advertising southern fried chicken, Drew pulled into the drive-thru window and ordered a bucket of chicken, potato salad, biscuits and drinks. The shrill sound coming from the intercom system on the display menu awakened Brie and she lifted her head from Drew's shoulder. After a moment of staring up at him in a sleepy daze, she asked, "Where are we?"

"I'm getting us some food. We can eat at my apartment," he explained gruffly, his voice hoarse from his inner struggle with two very powerful emotions—his unwanted, unequivocal desire for Brie, and his ever-growing anger toward himself for not having better control. "I have to go by my place to pick up some of the supplies we'll be needing."

"More food? But we just ate a few hours ago," Brie said, gingerly sliding to her side of the cab. She didn't have any idea how she'd gotten to his side in the first place.

Maybe he'd made a sharp left and she'd slid over. She sure hoped he didn't think she'd intentionally snuggled up to him.

"I ate. You didn't, remember? I sure as heck don't want you getting sick on me while we're out in the middle of nowhere. You'll be burning up a lot of energy once we reach the swamp."

"If that's where we're headed," Brie added. "But you don't know that for sure, yet."

"I'm 99.9 percent sure."

"Well, whatever," Brie stated. "You needn't worry about me. I'm a tough cookie."

Drew looked over at her, allowing his eyes to drop down the length of her and then back up again. "Sure you are," he replied, turning his attention toward easing his truck back onto the main road. "And kryptonite is your only weakness, right?"

"Right," Brie replied, nodding her head in agreement.

And then for some unknown reason, their eyes met and held. And as crazy as it would have sounded to someone who wasn't there, eternity seemed to reach out to them during that brief flash of time. But as quickly as it had come about, the spellbinding moment was gone and they both looked away.

A few minutes later they arrived at a two-story apartment complex. Entering Drew's apartment from the kitchen, he set the bucket of chicken on the dining table. "Let's eat while everything is still hot," he said, collecting two napkins, two forks and two plates from a cabinet and setting them down on the wicker place mats that were already in place. He motioned for Brie to sit down and she did. "Then I'll get the supplies down from upstairs."

Midway through the meal, Drew used a remote control to flick on a small-screen television that was placed on the counter near the microwave. He flipped to a channel giving the local weather. After they finished eating, Brie helped clear away the mess. Then Drew started for the stairs. Assuming she would help out, Brie followed behind him. "Where are the supplies?"

"Upstairs in the spare bedroom," Drew replied, halting at the foot of the staircase. He turned to face her. "This shouldn't take me long. So just have a seat."

"I'll help," Brie replied.

"I don't need your help."

"But I don't mind."

"But I do," Drew finally replied flatly. Then his voice softened. "So just have a seat, okay?"

So, his private world was upstairs, and he didn't want her there. Okay, no problem. She'd gotten the hint.

Marching to the sofa, Brie plopped down on the middle cushion. It might have taken her a while to get his drift, but now that she had, she could have cared less if he did all the work by himself. He didn't want her help? Fine. He wasn't getting it.

She didn't even bother to look his way when, from somewhere halfway up the stairs, she heard him say, *"Ah, the hell with everything."*

After the sound of Drew's footsteps on the stairs quieted and she heard him moving around upstairs, she slowly began to look around his living room. And much to her surprise, she found it to be tastefully decorated in the deep, rich colors of wine, cream and navy blue. Someone—she supposed a professional decorator—had carefully coordinated the oriental rug with all the other furnishings.

Then her gaze lifted to the stained oak mantel above the fireplace and that was when she noticed two framed black-and-white snapshots that were placed side by side. From where she sat she could see that one snapshot was of her grandfather and Drew. They were standing together as comrades would, smiling, with their arms placed across each other's shoulders. At their feet was an old treasure chest.

Her eyes wandered to the next snapshot and for a second she just stared, frozen in her seat. Because there before her, framed in silver, was a captured moment from her past. A moment long forgotten, but now instantly rekindled, and a sudden rush of emotion accompanied it.

Unconscious of her actions, Brie rose and walked to the mantel. The snapshot, undoubtedly, was one of a kind, a fluke, so to speak. A candid shot of her and her grandfather—the only one of its kind that she knew of—taken during the last visit he'd paid to her home in Georgia nine years ago. The photographer who had taken the photo had somehow managed to steal a rare moment in time that was never to be again.

"What are you doing?" Drew asked from right behind her, his deep voice causing Brie to jump.

Shaken, Brie hurriedly replaced the snapshot she hadn't realized she'd gotten up to hold, her hands trembling as she did so. "Nothing," she replied quickly.

Drew caught her chin with his fingers and turned her face toward his. One corner of his mouth lifted in a grin. "I'm sorry I surprised you. I didn't mean to."

Smiling gingerly, she pulled free of his hold and turned back to look at the pictures. Pointing to the first snapshot, the one of him and her grandfather, she said, "I like this one."

"Yeah, it's always been a favorite of mine, too. It was taken a few years ago in the West Indies."

"The two of you look quite pleased with yourselves," she said.

"Yeah ... well, we'd just found this treasure that we'd been looking for," Drew replied. "And I guess we were pretty full of ourselves at the time."

Brie lifted the snapshot. "You and my grandfather shared a lot together, didn't you?" she said, her gaze skimming across the mantel and coming to rest on the other snapshot.

"Yeah, we had some good times," Drew replied, suddenly feeling guilty for having shared all those good times with his old friend. He knew Brie was suffering from her grandfather's rejection. He even felt he understood what her childhood must have been like, with her constantly trying to win his attention. He remembered how it felt to be ignored.

And that was why, Drew reminded himself, it was better for a person like Duke—and like himself—someone who wasn't willing to love unconditionally, not to have a family. Too much was expected of a person. In those kinds of relationships, enough was never enough. If someone gave a hundred percent of himself, then two hundred was expected. Drew felt he knew how to take care of himself. But he damned sure didn't know the first thing about taking care of anyone else.

Simply put, he was nobody's keeper. And that was the way he liked it. That was why after all this was over, Brie had to make it on her own.

With his thoughts now back to the present, Drew noticed that Brie was still studying the two snapshots, her eyes glossed over with tears. "Brie," he began, placing his hand alongside her face. It certainly wasn't what he'd intended on saying—or doing, for that matter. But he watched in fascination as her light blue eyes widened in response to his touch. Then his gut tightened as her eyes met his and her lips began to tremble. A reaction, he knew, caused by the fact that he was now lowering his face toward hers.

What in the hell was he doing?

And then his mouth came down on hers, firmly. But even that didn't give him enough of what he wanted, and so his firmly applied pressure quickly turned hard—hot—and demanding. Even more demanding than the anger he felt toward himself for kissing her. He ignored his every warning and slipped his arms around her waist, pulling her firm body against his. He was hungry…starving for a taste of her.

Brie was indeed surprised by his sudden move, but not nearly as much as when she realized that her body was coming alive, tingling. Worse, she wanted—and was taking—every divine moment of pleasure he was willing to give her. A pleasure so savage in its complete control of her that it cannibalized her insides until she had nothing left but a raw, burning need to have the kiss last forever. She had, after all, waited nine long years for this moment.

Maybe that was why it was Drew who, only moments later, pulled away first, leaving Brie totally shaken and feeling like the foolish girl she'd once been. Breathless, refusing to met his gaze, she turned and hurried toward the downstairs bathroom. Once inside, she shut the door behind her and leaned against it. Now alone, she closed her eyes and unwillingly recalled the past few moments.

Still standing in the spot where she'd left him, Drew sucked in a deep calming breath.

All right, dammit, so this whole out-of-control situation was his doing. Okay. He would take the blame. Yes, he was guilty of instigating the kiss. But it was just a part of the game he was playing, he told himself firmly. And ordinarily—if not always—he was exceptionally good at playing life's little games. After all, he'd been playing them all of his life.

Well ... this time he'd let the game go too far. In fact, *way* too far. Therefore, he wanted out. This very minute. Before he became involved. Before he had himself actually convinced he needed her. And he wanted out without any more of a warning given to Brie than the one she'd gotten when he'd ended the kiss as abruptly as he had. Surely she'd gotten his message.

Obviously, though, he hadn't. Not if his pounding heart was any indication. Even his breathing was erratic and, yes, his thoughts were still reeling, grasping like tentacles at the delicious moments just passed, not wanting to let them go. And his gut was still knotted up, tight with the kind of ridiculous tension that had made him do something as crazy as kiss Brianna when he should have kept her at arm's length. Undoubtedly, if he'd bothered to ask for a spirit's intervention before kissing her, Duke would have spoken up and said that Drew was losing control.

And having control was absolutely necessary to him.

You're being too hard on yourself, his inner voice suddenly chimed in. *Yeah, sure, it's possible that Duke's frowning down at you right now. But don't forget, Drew, you didn't always agree with your old friend.*

Yeah, but Duke had lived his life without many regrets. And he had done it by remaining uncommitted to anyone other than himself. He'd lived his life his way, and that was how Drew wanted to do it, too. His way.

Ah ... to hell with everything, Drew finally told himself again, once more climbing the stairs. All he'd done was mess up a few measly seconds of his life. What was that in the overall scope of time? Hardly anything at all. Certainly not enough to get all worked up over. Before long, he wouldn't even remember this incident.

Yeah, right, his inner voice replied.

Moments later, after pulling herself together, Brie came out of the bathroom. Her emotional guards were back in place and no one—especially Drew—would ever suspect how turned inside out she had been for a while. Finding herself alone in the room where she'd left him, she spun around and headed for the kitchen, only to stop in the doorway when she heard a *thud* behind her. Glancing back over her shoulder, she saw a royal blue sleeping bag that someone—Drew, obviously—had tossed down from upstairs. A moment later another sleeping bag—this one red—came crashing down right next to the first one. Soon, a couple of pillows and several blankets followed. Finally, Brie heard the drumming of heavy footsteps as Drew descended the stairs. She looked up, saw him carrying a large box and quickly moved out of his way.

"What's all this?" she asked.

He set the box down on the floor in the kitchen near the back door. "Supplies." Then he started back upstairs.

"There's more?" she asked innocently, watching him climb.

"Yeah," Drew replied over his shoulder. "But not much. So just stay put."

"I wouldn't consider doing anything else," Brie replied dryly, feeling certain if he had needed help, he would not have wanted hers. Which was just fine with her. He hadn't wanted what she'd offered him nine years ago, either.

And maybe that was why she knew the kiss he'd given her earlier was nothing but a fluke. Something that had just happened. She was certain that it had meant nothing to him.

Within a couple of minutes, Drew came down with another box of supplies that he carried outside and loaded in his pickup. Then he came inside for the first one. This time Brie followed him to his truck, toting the two bedrolls, pillows and extra blanket. Once Drew was freed from his own load, he took them from her and tossed them in next to the other supplies.

"That's it for now," he said, slamming shut the tailgate. "After we get our hands on the map and find out exactly what direction we'll be heading, we might still need a few other things." Brushing his hands together, he added, "Go ahead and get in the truck while I lock up."

She did and before long he joined her. He drove by her motel so she could pick up her belongings and check out, then, after steering his pickup onto the main highway, he headed in the direction of Broussard, a small town just south of Lafayette. Several miles later, he made a right turn and started down a country road. Finally, he took a sharp left down a rutted dirt trail that was lined on both sides with tall, skinny pines. He told Brie the narrow pathway was leading them to her grandfather's home. But Brie couldn't imagine the makeshift road leading anywhere, much less to a house.

But within moments, they'd reached a clearing and he was pulling his truck to a stop. Between the bright moonlight and the headlights on the truck, Brie could see an old structure that looked abandoned, and she knew instantly that this was the house her great-grandfather Bernard had built for his bride a long, long time ago.

Brie was mesmerized, in spite of the fact that Drew hadn't exaggerated the deteriorating condition of the old place. As far as she could tell, the only visible evidence that the wood structure had ever been painted was along the front porch area, where there were still a few patches and chips of white paint scattered here and there.

After a moment, her gaze drifted from the house and skimmed across the grounds. Two moss-covered oaks were located on each corner of the long front porch, their cumbersome branches now sprawled in every direction across the yard, as though they had been given the ominous job of guarding the old house against possible trespassers.

And who knew? Maybe that *was* their job, Brie thought, her eyes gathering moisture in spite of the fact she'd just told herself she wasn't going to cry. It was only that she'd suddenly realized how the devastation of the old homestead was a representation of what her family heritage had become.

But surely, there had been laughter here once, Brie reassured herself as she breathed in deeply. Surely her great-grandfather who had supposedly built this house so long ago and with such joy, had built it with thoughts of his children and his grandchildren and great-grandchildren running and playing beneath the old trees. Brie had to believe that *he*, at least, had cared—that someone had cared. She wanted to believe that he and her great-grandmother had made it through life together and that, somewhere nearby, they had been laid to rest side by side, husband and wife, their legacy of everlasting love enshrined in marble for all eternity.

This is my home, Brie thought. Suddenly she realized that, at last, she'd truly found where she belonged—her very own roots—and that, no matter how far she ran now, she would never quite pull free of the binds that tied her to this old homestead. Never. But then, she didn't really want to. And now that she'd found her rightful place in this world, someday, somehow, she would return here to live out her days. It was her destiny—and had been all along.

Someday...somehow...she would find the laughter that had been lost here and she would bring it home again, forever.

Chapter Five

Hoping Drew hadn't noticed her emotional state, Brie turned her head away from him, and, with the back of her hand, quickly wiped at a couple of tears that had streaked down the sides of her cheeks. "Do you suppose my great-grandparents are buried near here?" she asked hopefully.

"I don't know, Brie," he replied quietly. "I haven't any idea where their graves are. Maybe they're in the same cemetery as your grandfather. He asked to be buried there, but he never said why—and I never thought to ask."

"Maybe so," she said, carefully keeping her still-wet gaze averted. She heard the door to Drew's side open.

"Getting out?" he inquired.

"Uh...yeah," she said, quickly sucking in a deep breath before opening the passenger door and stepping to the ground.

Gathering up her courage and going forward was what her great-grandparents would have expected of her. It was what she expected of herself.

With Drew automatically taking the lead, they approached the old house. Reaching the front porch, he became more cautious, pointing out several rotten boards with his flashlight and telling Brie to sidestep them. Once they were at the front door, he twisted the knob and found it was unlocked, which only indicated to Brie what little value the interior of the house must hold within its walls. Then, using his shoulder, Drew jarred loose the heavy oak door and pushed it open with a loud creak.

"I'll go in first," he said, shining his beam of light on the floor just ahead of his feet. He looked back at Brie and frowned. "The other flashlight I put between us on the seat of the truck, did you bring it with you?"

Brie quickly snapped on the orange-and-white canister-style flashlight. "I have it right here," she replied.

"Use it."

"Okay... I will," she said breathlessly, noting the irritation in his voice. But then, she really couldn't blame him. Obviously, they needed whatever source of light available to them, and here she was walking along behind him without turning on the flashlight he'd provided her. "Sorry."

"Never mind," he said gruffly, crossing the threshold in one stride. "Just watch your step." He stopped abruptly, almost causing Brie to run her face, flashlight and elbows completely through his back. Except for one long, frustrated sigh, he ignored the unexpected blow and continued to inspect the room they'd just entered, flicking his light from the floor to the ceiling. Then, in that nonchalant way of his, he said, "You know, Brianna, now's as good a time as any for you to remember the number one rule of survival."

Brie felt utterly clumsy for having slammed against him, and his insolent way of letting her know that she wasn't living up to his expectations only made her feel worse. She stepped back and rubbed the end of her smashed nose. "How could I possibly forget?" she muttered dryly.

Pivoting around, he flicked his flashlight down the length of her. "Are you all right?"

"Just about as hunky-dory as can be."

He flashed his light on her face, and narrowing his gaze, carefully scrutinized her every feature. "Didn't I warn you that this expedition wasn't going to be easy?" he asked in frustration. "Look, if you can't cut it here, then I've got news for you. This is nothing compared to what the actual hunt for Old Gabe's treasure is going to be like. In fact, I've just made a decision." He quickly dropped the eight-inch spotlight from her face. "I'm afraid I'm going to have to insist that you stay behind—and that's all there is to it."

"Oh, no, you don't. I'm not staying behind," Brie retorted. "We're in this together. Where you go, I go. And that's that."

"You don't seem to understand. It could mean your life."

"And not yours?"

He turned back around to explore the room. "I know how to survive in this world. You don't."

"And just what gives you the right to say that?" Brie asked haughtily.

"Because I wouldn't be in this damned mess in the first place if you did," he said over his shoulder.

Brie frowned. "Now what is *that* supposed to mean?"

"Nothing," Drew snapped, continuing his inspection. He scanned his light over the fireplace located on the wall opposite them. Two high-backed wooden rockers and one small round table were pulled to the front of it. "Besides," he added casually, "right now we've got more important things to worry about."

"Now wait one cotton-pickin' minute, Drew. I want to know what you meant by—"

"Look over there," he said suddenly, interrupting her. "Is that a rat?"

Rat? All thoughts of their previous discussion vacated Brie's mind. If he had meant to terrify her with his sudden outburst, then the guy deserved an Oscar for his performance. She was petrified—literally shaking at the knees. But before she could even react—as in run away—he grabbed her by the hand and forced her flashlight to shine alongside his. "No, it's just an old sock, or something—I think."

"You think?" Brie sputtered, her voice sounding shrill. Scrunching up her toes, she huddled up as close to him as she possibly could. If there had been enough room inside, she would have liked nothing better at that moment than to cram herself into one of his pockets, preferably his shirt pocket, which for now would put her where she wanted to be most—the farthest point possible from the floor.

"It's nothing, Brie."

Still close to him, she said, "That's easy for you to say. You're wearing boots. I've got on flats."

Drew whirled and darted his light down to her feet. "You mean you're not wearing boots?"

"No," Brie replied.

"Why not, for heaven's sake? Didn't you buy a pair at the wilderness store like I told you to?"

Brie grimaced at the anger in his voice. "Yes . . . I just forgot to put them on."

Suddenly she found herself being whisked up in Drew's arms. Surprised by his actions, she clutched the orange-and-white flashlight to her breasts and held on to it for dear life. However, by the time he'd stepped off the front porch and was marching toward his truck, she'd found her voice. "What are you doing?" she asked bluntly.

Drew sighed heavily. "The number one rule of survival has a preface," he said through clenched teeth. "Obviously, I failed to mention that to you."

"Obviously," Brie replied dryly, not allowing herself to become totally upset with his overbearing behavior. In a way, she'd probably asked for some of the anger that was spewing from him. She *had* forgotten to wear her boots, which undoubtedly would have given her feet and lower legs more protection than the skimpy shoes she was wearing. Still, her patience with his arrogant behavior was quickly wearing down to the thickness of air. "Well? What are you going to do now?"

His mouth formed a hard line. "I'm going to try—one more time—to make you understand something. The number one rule of survival is simple—take care of yourself. The preface to this simple rule states that one must *come prepared* to take care of oneself," he said testily. "Do you think you can get that through your skull?"

Trying her best to keep her sense of humor, Brie clicked her tongue twice. "Got it, sir, Master Sergeant, sir."

Drew's features stilled. "This is serious, Brianna. You've got to dress alert, act alert, be alert."

"To what?" Brie asked, now more than just a bit piqued, herself. She wasn't a child, and she didn't appreciate his treating her as if she were his responsibility. "We're at my grandfather's house, for heaven's sake, not in some jungle treehouse. Is this pitiful, run-down old place your grand idea of danger? Because if it is, I've got news for you..."

Still clutched within his arms, Brie saw when his jaw went tight and a look of pure frustration seized hold of his features. "No—dammit, this place isn't my 'grand idea' of danger. But this sure as hell is," he growled. Within a split second, his lips came down on hers—hard.

The bruising kiss lasted but a moment. Then he pulled away and glared at her with angry and hungry eyes that kept hers glued to his. Finally, he said, "Sometimes, Brianna, you scare the hell out of me."

Her eyes widened slightly. "Sometimes you scare the hell out of me, too," she replied.

And then he was kissing her again, only this time when his lips took hers, they weren't at all punishing.

This time it was Brie who pulled away, only to find herself staring into his smothering gaze, searching for some clue as to what was happening between them. But when she realized that she was only jeopardizing the mood of the moment, she quickly slipped her arm around his neck and forced his head down to hers. Drew groaned in obvious surprise when she opened her mouth against his.

And then they both discovered a mutual hunger, so urgent and straightforward in its target that it consumed them totally, mercilessly, slashing away at their emotional guards, leaving them defenseless.

But as time marched forward, they came to their senses at the same moment, or so it seemed, and they jerked apart as though they were two negative forces, repelling each other. Drew allowed Brie to slide down the length of him until she was standing on her own two feet. And then, without further comment, he quickly dropped his hold from around her waist, turned and hurried off into the darkness, leaving Brie staring after him.

But he'd had no choice.

Determined to handle the situation in his own way, Drew made several long strides to the back of the house where he could be alone...where he could savor the hard, solid earth beneath his feet and forget that for one tiny second he'd floated aimlessly beyond any kind of human control. Because during that one fleeting moment, he'd wanted Brie and the peace he'd felt she could bring to his soul more than anything. Even more than he'd wanted his freedom.

Unaware of his surroundings, he rested one shoulder against a corner post of an old rose arbor that had been neglected for too many years and was now overgrown with evergreen vines. After cocking back his hat, he found himself reaching into his T-shirt pocket for a pack of cigarettes, a habit he'd stopped nearly ten years ago. Realizing what he'd just done, he cursed, took a deep breath, kicked at a pinecone on the ground and sent it sailing off into the dark night. Then his long, restless fingers slipped into the back pockets of his worn blue denim jeans, and for the first time since old Duke died, he stared up at the starry sky and wondered if his good friend somehow knew of the mess he'd created. Then Drew thought about Brie and the way she'd felt in his arms only moments ago. He could still taste her sweetness. He'd told her that she scared him. But the truth was, it wasn't Brie he was frightened of. It was himself—and his damned lack of control when he was near her.

For a long while, he just stood there with his hands in his back pockets, gazing into the darkness as he wrestled with his wrung-out feelings. For the first time in a long time, he thought—really thought—about life and death and being alone. Unfortunately for him, his thoughts on the matter didn't go down quite as easily as they always had in the past. In fact, for one tiny frightening second, the part about being alone stuck like a knife in the pit of his stomach. But only for a second. Then he quickly swallowed the doubts he'd unwillingly conjured for himself. After all, being alone was merely a state of mind. For one thing, there was a big difference between being alone and being lonely. And for the moment, at least, the explanation of a self-induced aloneness seemed to help ease the dull pain in his chest.

When Drew finally strolled back to the front of the house, he found Brie sitting inside his truck, her back poised rigidly for his viewing. Because she'd left the passenger door open, he could see that one of her legs was hiked up on the seat. Clearly, she had no intentions of trying to help ease the awkwardness that was now sure to exist between them because of that one, darn out-of-control kiss. Obviously, she'd decided to remain true-blue to her female gender and give him the cold shoulder routine. Well, so be it, Drew told himself. Because now that he was back in control of himself, he could make things pretty darn difficult for her, too.

Wanting to make sure he'd gain Brie's full attention before speaking, Drew cleared his throat. "Look, just to set the record straight, what happened between us a while ago is never going to happen again. It was a stupid thing for me to do, and I don't happen to like being stupid. So let's forget about it and go on with what it is we have to do." Then, feeling as though he'd just given them both a valid reason to ignore the whole incident, he hesitated, waiting for her to respond. He was gravely disappointed when she didn't give him the slightest benefit of an answer—not even so much as a twitch of a jaw muscle.

But Drew wasn't a man who was easily discouraged. He cleared his throat again. "So now that I've solved that little detail, it's time to get down to business," he said. "Therefore—" he eyed her back irritably "—I'll get the sleeping bags and supplies from the truck while you..." He paused before reaching into the back of the pickup for the items he'd mentioned, giving her what he considered ample time to make some attempt to cooperate with him. But when she still didn't make a move—suddenly, impulsively, and because her posture was simply too haughty for him to tolerate a moment longer—he grabbed her by the waist and whirled her around so she would have no choice but to meet his glare. "You, Miss Stansbury, need to stop acting like a child and, for your own safety, get your boots on your feet this minute. And don't bother me with some silly, redundant question like *Why?* because I'm in no mood to answer it."

She was tempted. Lord only knew, how much she was tempted. That simple, three-letter word he'd dared her to say throbbed on the end of her tongue. *Go ahead, say it,* her inner voice chimed.

Brie opened her mouth to speak but nothing came out. Oh, what the heck, she told herself. She wasn't in the mood to fight with him, anyway. So, instead, she gave him a stiff salute and said, "Yes, sir, Master Sergeant, sir."

Drew smiled cynically. "Well, it looks like you're finally coming around to my way of thinking. Good girl. It's about time."

"Go to hell, Drew Naquin. Who put you in charge, anyway?"

"I guess your grandfather did."

She hopped out of the truck. "Bull. You put yourself in charge."

"Are you suggesting that you should be the head of this operation?"

"Well . . . yes—no."

"Well . . . ?" Drew replied with a smirk, placing his hands on his hips. "Which is it going to be? Yes or no?"

"You know the answer to that. Of course I can't be in charge. I don't have the experience you do."

"Then we agree that I'm in charge, right?"

Brie sighed heavily. "Yes. You're in charge."

"Good." He turned then and began rummaging through their supplies. When he found what he was looking for, he whirled and said, "Here, get these on your feet before some big oversize nutria comes along and bites off your toes—oh, and by the way, be sure to keep them on until I say otherwise."

"But won't we be turning in soon for the night?" Brie asked innocently.

Drew eyes met hers, hard and unrelenting. "It doesn't make any difference. You'll be sleeping with your boots on, anyway."

"I will? But why?" Brie responded, shivering from a gust of cold air that seeped through the thin fabric of her clothing. She wrapped her arms around her middle in the hopes of warming herself against the chills that lingered. It felt as if the temperature had suddenly dropped ten degrees. But when she looked up and saw the sober expression on Drew's face, the changing weather became the least of her worries.

Oh-oh, she'd said that three-letter word, after all.

Drew sucked in a lungful of crisp air. "Because if you don't, and the bogeyman doesn't get 'em first, your little toesies will undoubtedly freeze off during the night."

Brie smiled brightly. "See? That wasn't so hard a question to answer, now, was it?"

"Just get the boots on your feet. *Please*," he added with emphasis.

"I will," she replied with an enthusiastic shake of her head. After all, she'd asked a simple question and the man had given her his answer. And to his credit, he'd made his point perfectly clear. Besides, she didn't know why she was giving him such a hard time about something so trivial. Maybe it was her way of trying to keep some distance between them. Nonetheless, she certainly had no intention of letting herself freeze. She opened the rectangular cardboard box he'd shoved into her hands, donned a new pair of white athletic socks and then worked her feet into her brand-new hiking boots. It took her several minutes to get them laced up.

While doing so, her thoughts turned back to the weather. She hadn't realized that it was going to get this cold tonight. One reason, she supposed, was that she'd had so much on her mind lately, she hadn't been paying much attention to the forecasts. Another was that she'd never been this cold in her entire life, and it was hard for her to imagine herself in this kind of a predicament. Oh, sure, she'd been in freezing temperatures before. But always before, when that had happened to her, there had been blankets and heaters, or fireplaces and hot chocolate waiting nearby to warm her chilled body. The plain truth was she'd never stayed outdoors overnight in her life. Not ever.

Well . . . maybe once . . . if her best friend's fifth grade slumber party counted for something. But to her recollection, that night wasn't anything like this. For one thing, the slumber party had taken place in midsummer, when the temperature was hot and humid. Her friend's father had pitched a pup tent for them on the patio in the backyard and had used a heavy-duty extension cord to set up a light on the inside so the girls could see one another. For entertainment, they'd even had a small television set. But tonight she wasn't even sure if she would have a decent pillow under her head. And while she and her best friend had slept in matching oversize T-shirts with a big black-and-white panda bear decal on the front, Drew was making it sound as if she'd be eaten alive before morning by a real bear if she didn't bundle up every single inch of herself. Not only that, but he had her imagining that some form of danger lurked in every dark corner of her grandfather's run-down house. Frankly, she was beginning to wish she'd stayed in her motel room for the night. At least there she would have had a warm shower, and a soft, cozy bed to sleep in. And, too, there wouldn't have been anyone with her who had the temperament of a marine drill sergeant.

Maybe Drew was correct, after all. Maybe going on this treasure hunt with him was biting off more than she could chew. Maybe she *was* too much a city girl, though, Lord knew, she hated having to admit that. But one thing was for sure. If she was willing to go as far as to admit defeat, then she would have to go all the way and be completely honest with herself about her reason for giving up. Which meant that she would have to accept the fact that it had more to do with trying to distance herself from Drew than it did with her running away from some poor little creature scurrying around in the dark, looking for food. Because if she'd learned anything at all since arriving in Louisiana, it was that Drew Naquin somehow posed a far greater threat to her well-being than any beast—big or small—ever would.

So maybe it was time she reconsidered her hasty decision to go with him. After all, she had nothing to gain by it. Dear God . . . it was *his* life that was at stake. . . .

Drew walked up to Brie, carrying a lighted lantern. "Here," he said, handing it to her, "keep this with you while I go around back to gather some firewood." He turned to walk away.

"Drew?"

"Yeah?" he asked, easily throwing back the reply over his shoulder.

"Please be careful," Brie said softly.

He turned around slowly, a bemused expression on his face.

Brie gave him a small grin. "I know you don't like me to mention the loan shark and all, but I haven't forgotten about the threat he presents to you. I just hope you haven't, either."

Something seemed to squeeze the air from Drew's lungs. "No, Brie, I haven't forgotten about him." He took two steps toward her, then came to an instant halt, staring down at the ground for what seemed like endless moments. Finally, he looked up again and Brie could tell by his expression that whatever his original intentions had been, he'd changed his mind. "Look, it's not me you need to be worrying about. Remember what I said about the number one rule—"

"Of survival," Brie cut in testily. "Yes, yes, I remember every single word of it."

Drew frowned at her. "Just stay put until I get back. No sight-seeing on your own, understood?"

Brie glared at him sourly. "I haven't any intentions of venturing off by myself."

"Is that a promise?" he asked.

"It's a statement."

"Then I need a promise from you that you will remain right here until I return."

"Okay," she replied.

He waited. "Okay, what?"

"Okay. I promise."

"Good," Drew said. Then he pivoted on his heels and quickly disappeared into the vast darkness surrounding them.

Shivering after another gust of cold wind proved to be too much for just her long-sleeved shirt, Brie reached inside the cab of the truck for the extra parka. Drew had brought it along from his apartment after he'd asked her if she had a coat with her and she'd told him that she hadn't bothered to pack one when she'd left Atlanta. Thank goodness he'd thought to ask, because she certainly was in need of the added warmth the downy jacket would give her. In fact, after slipping into it, she didn't mind that its sleeves were too long, or that its wide elastic band that should have gathered at her waist hung to her hips. Being oversize only meant it blanketed all the more of her goosefleshy body. She felt cozier and somehow safe snuggled within its thick, soft wall of insulation. In fact, she was feeling so much better now, she was beginning to wonder if maybe she hadn't overreacted earlier when she'd questioned her ability to cope with her impending circumstances. Maybe she'd been willing to throw in the towel too soon. Why, wasn't it only two weeks ago that she'd managed to put a certain renowned gigolo in his place? she reminded herself, now feeling more and more confident with her own resourcefulness as each second passed.

And then Brie couldn't help herself. She smiled. Because from somewhere deep down inside, she knew that she'd never really given up on herself in the first place. And she knew that simply because she knew she wasn't a quitter. In fact, Mr. Drew Naquin was going to be in for one big surprise. She *was* a tough cookie. Before all was said and done and she boarded a flight back to Atlanta, she was going to make sure he knew it, too. Call it pride, but whenever it came time for her to leave Louisiana, she planned on taking back with her one thing of value. And that was Drew Naquin's respect.

In less than five minutes Drew was back with an armload of branches. He went inside the house and came out empty-handed. "I'll be right back," he said, slipping into the darkness. Within a few seconds, he returned with another load of wood.

Allowing the lantern he'd given her to light her path, Brie followed Drew inside and saw he'd dumped the first stack of branches inside the fireplace. She watched as he placed the other one nearby. Then he crouched, lighted a match and strategically placed it against the pile inside the hearth. After tossing in a couple of pinecones, he brushed off his hands and waited for them to catch fire. They did, and soon there was a small blaze going. Rising to his full height, he said, "Get over here, Brie, and warm up."

Drew didn't have to tell Brie twice. She set the lantern on the floor and within a split second, she was standing beside him, her arms outstretched toward the crackling fire. "Ohh . . . this feels good!" she exclaimed.

Grinning, Drew took a step back and sized her up. "Nice jacket," he said.

His comment generated a playful mood in Brie and she immediately pretended to be modeling the coat for his benefit. "Oversize is in vogue this year," she said, the corners of her mouth tilting upward. She slipped her hands under the fold-down collar and lifted it so that it hugged the sides of her face. Then she tucked her hands into the side pockets and turned so he could view the loose fit from all sides.

"Nice. Very nice," Drew added with a twinkle in his eyes. He reached out to adjust one corner of the collar, touching her cheek in the process, and it seemed to Brie that his fingers lingered a moment longer than necessary. She wasn't sure what he was up to—maybe he was just going along with the game she'd started—but the feel of his fingers caressing her skin, however slight, had her heart pumping frantically.

He dropped his hand to his side. Tucking his fingertips into his jean pockets, he started for the door. "Stay here. I've got to gather some more wood to last the night. But that shouldn't be a problem. I saw plenty on the ground out back."

"I can help," Brie replied meaningfully.

Hesitating but a moment, he said, "Okay, get the sleeping bags from the truck, bring them in here and get them ready for bedding down."

"Where should I put them?" she asked.

"Near the fire, Brie," he answered in an exasperated voice as he went out the door shaking his head.

Brie grimaced at her own stupidity. "Of course, dodo brain," she said out loud to herself. Boy, but was it ever obvious that she'd never earned any scouting medals. Nor would she ever, if she continued at the rate she was going. Undoubtedly, if she had joined Girl Scouts, the skills she would have learned would have come in handy today.

Frankly, she couldn't think of any reason that she *hadn't* participated in scouting. She wouldn't be too terribly surprised, however, if she were to think back to her youth and recall that it was her grandmother who had discouraged her. Brie knew she'd missed out on a lot of other fun, worthwhile things while growing up because of her aging grandmother's overprotectiveness.

She scrambled out to the truck, retrieved the bedrolls, pillows and blankets and hurried back inside. She laid out the blue sleeping bag first, placing it vertical to the fireplace. She did the same with the red one, leaving about three feet of space between them. She would have left more room but that would have placed one of the bedrolls too far from the warmth of the fire. She certainly had no intention of sleeping right next to Drew, but she certainly had no intention of freezing all night long, either. She tossed a pillow and a blanket on top of each. Then she stood with her back to the fire, her hands folded behind her, and pictured the long hours that awaited her until morning. Suddenly the floor seemed awfully hard, in spite of the plush sleeping bag, and the room seemed awfully cold, in spite of the blazing fire. Once inside her bedroll, how was she going to keep her head and her feet warm all at the same time?

Suddenly, using his shoulder, Drew barreled through the front door with another armload of wood. He dumped it alongside the one near the fireplace and spun around to head outside again.

"Don't you think you've gathered enough branches to last the night?" Brie asked.

Drew glanced at the small woodpile. "Maybe. But while I'm at it, I'd rather gather extra, just to be sure. I can tell you right now that it won't be much fun if one of us has to crawl out of our warm sleeping bag at three o'clock in the morning to go in search of more wood."

A shiver ran down Brie's spine. "I suspect you're right about that," she replied without any argument. Feeling guilty that she wasn't outside helping him, she started to follow. But after only two steps, he seemed to sense her intentions and spun around.

"If you really want to help out," he said, "then stay put. It's easier for me to gather firewood alone than to have to be worrying about you wandering off in the darkness and getting lost."

So that was his problem, Brie thought. Good grief, she might have not been Betsy Girl Scout, but she wasn't a lamebrain, either. "Believe it or not, I've been finding my way through Atlanta for years now. And for your information, Atlanta is a big city that's chock-full of twists and turns."

"But Atlanta isn't like these piney woods, where everything looks the same and the night is so pitch black that you can't see your fingers in front of your eyes. There's bayous and snakes—and some people even claim that there's quicksand, though I've never seen any. There's—"

"Okay," Brie cut in, breathing deeply. "You've made your point. I'll stay put."

Drew gazed at her, his eyes darkening. "I'm sorry. I guess that was a bit of overkill. It's just I don't want anything to happen to you," he said, his voice growing hoarse.

"Well, I don't want anything to happen to you, either," Brie replied, her breath catching in her throat. Just the thought of him being harmed . . . For one fleeting moment, she was almost tempted to toss her pride to the wind and throw herself into his arms in much the same fashion she had as a silly young girl. Only she was a woman now and her guards were in place, preventing her from making a complete fool of herself. No, sirree, she wasn't going to be anyone's fool ever again.

Drew shrugged. "I mean, it's only . . . well, I feel I owe your grandfather that much.

What a slap in the face! He wanted her safe because he felt he owed her grandfather.

Her emotional guards immediately lifted their extra shields to protect her from any additional pain. "Well, I know for a fact," Brie said, "that you would be the last person on this earth my grandfather would have wanted harmed. He loved you like a son."

"He loved you, too, Brie."

"Really?" she replied, calling to attention every ounce of courage she possessed. "Well, I guess I'll just have to take your word for that, now, won't I?"

"Yeah—for now, anyway," he replied, "But maybe someday soon you'll see things differently."

Quick, hot tears sprang to Brie's eyes, and after turning away from Drew so he wouldn't notice them, she headed toward the fireplace. Lord knew, she wished she could have seen things differently where her grandfather was concerned. But the truth was, years of evidence had shown her the reality of his feelings for her, as well as his feelings for her mother and grandmother. It was something she simply had to accept. Somehow.

And maybe someday she would.

In truth, for her own good, she had to believe that the day would come when she no longer had any tears to shed over the past.

Brie heard when Drew went out the door, shutting it behind him. Wiping at the moisture on her cheeks with the sleeve of her—his—parka, she knelt in front of the hot fire and let herself become mesmerized by its flickering flames. Then, probably because her thoughts drifted back to when she was a little girl and her grandmother would rock her for hours by the fireplace in their home, she recalled the look of sadness she'd always seen in her grandmother's eyes whenever the old woman was unaware that she was being observed. The realization that her grandmother's love—or, for that matter, any woman's love for a man—could survive in spite of the pain it caused them was disturbing, actually, downright frightening.

Therefore, taking a deep, calming breath, Brie reaffirmed the promise she'd made to herself. She *was not* going to love a man insanely like her grandmother had.

No man was worth that kind of misery. Not the man who had fathered her and then left town soon after marrying her mother. Not her adventurous grandfather who had simply ignored the love she'd given him. And certainly not Drew Naquin, who had the nerve to say he wanted her kept safe and sound only because he felt he owed her grandfather.

Chapter Six

Drew returned a few minutes later and dumped the last batch of wood he'd gathered from outdoors on the floor near the other piles. Then he picked up a couple of medium-size branches, tossed them into the flickering flames and watched until they started to burn.

"There," he said, rubbing his hands together. "That ought to keep the fire going for a while." For the next few minutes, he stood at the hearth and warmed himself. Finally, gesturing with a toss of his head toward the door leading into the next room, he said, "Wanna see what the rest of the house looks like?"

"Sure," Brie replied, jolting her thoughts back to the present. Shocked to discover that for one short moment she had somehow forgotten herself and had been admiring his rakish good looks, she blinked twice in an effort to shoo away the unwanted thoughts.

Wasn't it enough that her heart teetered on the brink of being lost to him forever, did her mind have to be foolish enough to want to follow along?

No way.

Determined more than ever to keep her brain on other matters—*any* other matters—Brie took a deep, steadying breath, folded her arms across her middle and moved several feet away from Drew.

First off, she did have other, much more important, matters to think about. He'd asked if she wanted to see the rest of the house. Well, the answer to that question was a definite yes, of course, she did. Actually, she was dying to see it. After all, this place belonged to her now. And while at times her brain still found it difficult to grasp that her grandfather had willed his home to her, her heart believed—wholeheartedly. "You're probably going to think I'm crazy when I say this, but I think I'm in love with this old house."

"Yeah, maybe just a little," Drew said with a shake of his head, giving the semidarkened room a slow once-over inspection. "It's not exactly a paradise, that's for sure. No one's bothered with its care in years."

"I know," Brie said, turning to study the wall next to her. Sighing, she slowly traced her fingertip down one of its many cracks. "Look, I know this house is nothing compared to the luxurious condos of today. But I bet it was once a nice place to live."

Narrowing his eyes, Drew examined the structural build. "Maybe so. But compared to today's standards, the construction is rather crude."

"Well," Brie protested, her posture stiffening, "of course its construction is crude. My great-grandfather Bernard built this house sometime before the Great Depression. And, according to my grandmother—who, by the way, was the only person who ever bothered to tell me anything about the Bernard family—my great-grandfather was a farmer, not a carpenter. Obviously, he did the best he could. And to be perfectly frank, I think the house is charming just the way it is."

"Look, I'm sorry. I didn't mean to sound critical. I was simply giving my opinion. And all I meant to say was that it will take a lot of work—and a lot of money—to restore this place to meet the building codes of today."

"Nonetheless," Brie stated, still feeling the need to defend her inheritance, "I might very well do exactly that someday."

Drew held up his hands in surrender. "Hey, be my guest. It's no hide off my back."

"That's right," Brie replied, straightening her shoulders.

Giving an exasperated sigh, Drew pivoted so that he no longer faced the blazing heat. Folding his hands behind his back, he asked, "Well, do you want to see the place, or not?"

Brie frowned. "You mean right now? Before morning...?"

"Yeah, why not?" he insisted, a sudden twinkle in his eyes. "I thought you might be interested in knowing what other guests could be joining us for the night."

"Other guests?" Brie repeated, her attention suddenly perking up. "What other guests?"

"Ah...now there lies the question," he said, his tone of voice suddenly becoming suspiciously ghoulish. Then he gave a low, mocking laugh. One that wasted no time in sending cold shivers down Brie's spine. "What other guests, indeed?" he continued, walking toward her and pretending to drag one leg behind him as if he were crippled. Then he curled his hands and fingers out in front of him until they looked as though they belonged to some crazed monster from an old Boris Karloff horror movie.

Another chill tingled down Brie's spine. However, as disquieted as she was by his weird behavior, she scowled at him. "Will you stop speaking in a voice that sounds like it once belonged to Edgar Allen Poe? And will you please stop pretending to be the Hunchback of Notre Dame? You're giving me the creeps, for heaven's sake. What's with you, anyway?"

Immediately backing off from his playful, though somewhat forbidding game, Drew relaxed his menacing pose. "Sorry if I scared you," he said, giving her a regular, good-old-fashioned, all-American grin. It brought her a tidal wave of relief—and also a slight quivering in the pit of her stomach. "But at least it worked," he added.

"What worked?"

"I was trying to lighten your mood."

"Lighten my mood?" Brie repeated with an exasperated smirk. "You had me downright spooked."

Drew grinned. "I was that good, huh?"

"Well—yeah—in a way," Brie replied, hating to admit that she'd been so easily intimidated by his performance. In fact, she fleetingly wondered if she shouldn't have been just a bit angry with him, but for some reason—maybe because of that silly-looking grin he was giving her—she couldn't seem to muster up the needed emotions.

After chuckling to himself, Drew said, "Duke and I used to do that kind of stuff all the time."

"Do what kind of stuff?"

For a couple of seconds, Drew's expression became distant. Then a slight smile returned to his face. "Old Duke and I used to like to joke around with the new guys who would come along with us on expedition. We'd tell them stories about mummies, curses, voodoo, *feu follets*—warlocks—just about anything, depending on the area folk-lore. And sometimes we'd get into the act of things. Just in fun, of course."

"In other words, you deliberately frightened your sub-ordinates."

"Well . . . we never thought of it that way, but—yeah, I guess you could say that was our intention," he confessed with a carefree shrug. "But I think it would be even more to the point if I said that we sometimes tried our darned-est to scare the pants off 'em."

"That's terrible!" Brie exclaimed.

Drew picked up a thick, long black rod that had been left on the floor near the fireplace and used it to poke at the blazing logs. "You don't understand, Brie. It wasn't like that. Hey, look—we're talking about grown men here, not frightened little boys. We were just having some fun around the campfire, that's all."

"Well, grown men or not," Brie said, "having your clothes scared off at any age doesn't sound like much fun to me."

"That's 'cause you're a woman, and men and women sometimes have different ideas about fun. Look, no one ever took anything we said or did really serious. They knew we were just trying to pass the time."

"Well, if you don't mind, I'd like to keep my pants on during this—or any—expedition," Brie countered, walk-ing toward a window where a pair of dingy-looking sheers hung, discolored with age and from a thick coating of dust that had long since settled into the fabric.

"And what if I do mind?" Drew asked.

It was probably the rough sound of his voice, or maybe it was the way his words seemed to hang in midair that caused Brie to whirl before she completely finished pro-cessing the insinuating question. But the instant she did, she prepared herself to meet the cocky expression she felt sure would be on his face.

Instead, she found herself targeted by a lopsided grin, and, because she hadn't taken any precautions against such a devious attack on his part, it succeeded in knocking down her emotional guards, leaving her momentarily defenseless. And before she could even regroup her army and counterattack, that same boyish grin slam-dunked her heart right into her stomach and the two organs went spiraling down to her knees.

That one casualty was severe. Surrender seemed her only option.

Now totally disarmed, Brie suddenly realized a shocking truth. That even with all of the warnings she'd given herself, it would still have been so easy for her to forget about picking up her guards for another battle and just surrender to him. So easy... and so much what she would have wanted to do in that moment—just as she'd always wanted to do during her weaker moments, when it had seemed pointless of her to fight against a need that never lessened or went away. It was only during her very weakest of moments that her desire for Drew could temporarily overpower her common sense and manifest itself as her strongest and only need in the whole wide world.

Which at any given time, Brie knew was an utterly ridiculous—downright dangerous—thing for her to let happen to herself. She'd be a complete fool to surrender her heart to a man who had made it painfully clear to her nine years ago that he didn't want it. Surrendering was out of the question.

Straightening her shoulders, Brie turned her eyes away from Drew. She didn't know what his game was now, but after the way she'd acted all those years ago, she wanted to make sure he understood that she was no longer a willing player in any kind of game. Things had changed over the years. *She* had changed. She was grown up now. She would put her emotional guards back in place, and this time, she would make sure they were secure enough to take any kind of attack.

Brie quickly gathered her courage, then without actually looking in Drew's direction, watched from the corner of her eye as he sauntered over to the lantern that she had set on the plank floor near the middle of the room. Lifting it, he held it up high with one hand so that its light illuminated the room. "Ready to explore?" he asked.

"I'll follow you," Brie replied, quickly falling in line behind him. When he looked at her suspiciously, she added, "Well, aren't you the head of this operation?"

Drew gazed at her as though he suddenly didn't trust one single cell in her body. "Yeah, I am. So, what's the deal?"

"No deal. Lead the way."

"Why?"

"Why what?"

"Why are you suddenly so cooperative?"

"No reason," she exclaimed, but for just a moment her eyes shot past him to peer into the darkness of the next room.

Responding, Drew glanced, too. Then he faced her again, this time with an all-knowing smile. "Too chicken to go first?"

"No," she replied, suddenly finding herself smiling back at him in spite of herself. Good Lord, but it would be so easy for her to let go.... "Just being cautious."

"You sure that's all?"

"I'm sure," she replied with a careless shrug. "And besides," she continued, feeling almost giddy inside—his smile was drugging her—"in order to call oneself the leader of a group, one must go first, right?"

"Right," he said sportively. "I knew you'd catch on to who's the boss, sooner or later."

"Oooh," Brie gasped, giving his shoulder a spontaneous, playful punch with her fist. "You're exasperating, Drew Naquin."

He studied her features. "And you're a lot of fun when you forget about being sad."

Brie instantly sobered. "Life can't always be fun and games."

"But it shouldn't always be sad, either."

"I never said it was."

"Life's what you make of it."

"Oh, please," Brie replied. "I don't need a lecture on the subject from someone who thinks every day needs to be a new adventure."

"Every day *is* a new adventure."

"Not in my life, thank God."

"What is it you expect from me, Brie? A damned apology because I happen to want a bigger kick out of life than you do?"

"I'm Duke Bernard's granddaughter, remember? I learned not to expect a thing from a man whose heart is always on a roller-coaster ride. It's a sure bet that he won't have time to care about anyone but himself."

Suddenly the lantern Drew carried was at his feet, and he was grabbing Brie by the shoulders and shaking her. "Take a good look at me, Brianna. *I'm not your grandfather.* It's time you separate the two of us in your mind and stop being angry with me because of something you feel he did to you and your family."

Startled by his quick movement, Brie could only gape at him. Finally, though, she managed to jerk herself free of his hold. "You've got it all wrong," she retorted, taking a step back. "I'm not angry at my grandfather because of what he did to me. I'm angry because of what he *didn't* do. He didn't love me—or my mother, or my grandmother—and he should have," she said, fighting back a sob that rose to her throat. But in spite of her efforts, her eyes still glistened with tears. "My grandmother went to her grave loving him. My mother did some wild and crazy things in her short life in the hopes of getting his attention and ended up dying at a tragically young age as a result. I tried to get his attention, too, but nothing I did was ever good enough. What was wrong with us? Why couldn't he have at least tried to love us back?"

Without waiting to second-guess his reasons for doing so, Drew suddenly wrapped his arms around Brie and pulled her against him. But the truth was, he couldn't help himself. His heart had gone out to her and the rest of him had followed automatically—pronto. She had needed comforting, and he, as strange as it sounded even to his own ears, had wanted to give it to her. Actually, he had needed to give it to her.

But, it wasn't the strong, defiant woman Brie presented to the world, the one who was proving herself to be quite a fighter, that he felt the need to comfort. That woman was capable of taking care of herself. It was the other woman, the vulnerable one, the one Brie kept hidden from everyone, that was presently tugging at his heartstrings. That woman wasn't cynical, or sophisticated, or even a fighter. He'd watched that woman lovingly place a bouquet of daisies on the grave of a man who had caused her nothing but pain and disappointment. He'd watched her wipe away her tears for him. In essence, that woman was like a hurt little girl, teary-eyed and frightened, even if she didn't re-alize that about herself. But like a trusting child, that woman was still looking for answers to questions that could no longer be answered. Sooner or later, she would have to give up the crusade and just get on with her life. But until she did, she would keep on hurting as she was doing now.

And, dammit, like a fool, he would probably want to keep on comforting her.

"Look," he found himself saying as he gently rubbed the center of her back in a circular motion, "it wasn't your fault. It wasn't anyone's fault but Duke's. He had too much pride."

"What did pride have to do with his loving us?" Brie asked, sniffing once as she pulled away just enough to look up into Drew's face.

When he gazed down at her, it seemed to Drew that the blue of her eyes was struggling to stay afloat in a sea of glistening tears. And for one brief second, he thought the sweet innocence of that look had stopped his heart from beating. But, fortunately for him, he quickly realized that it was only the rhythm that had been altered. He inhaled deeply. "Duke only talked about what happened between him and your grandmother once—and even that time was pretty brief. He said he came home from one of his expeditions and she had packed up your mother and all their belongings and had gone back to Georgia."

"Do you blame her? He was always gone, and most of the time, if she needed him, she didn't know where to look."

"I'm not blaming anybody," Drew exclaimed. "But did you know that he went after her with the intention of bringing her and your mother back to Louisiana? He said he'd made up his mind to settling down."

Brie looked skeptical. "No. No one ever told me that."

"Doesn't it kind of surprise you that your grandmother never told you anything like that?"

Brie nodded. "Kind of.... Well...yes...certainly, it would have made a difference to her...."

"I wonder if she even knew," Drew replied.

"But if he came for her," Brie persisted, "surely she knew."

"Not necessarily," Drew said. "Duke said that before he even got to the family home that day, he was confronted by your grandmother's father and a couple of her uncles. They told him that your grandmother didn't want him anymore, not under any circumstances. They said she was being courted by someone else—some local kid who was going to college to be a medical doctor. Back in the early forties that was considered quite an accomplishment. They told him that this guy wanted to marry her and that she had started divorce proceedings against him. Then they ridiculed your grandfather as being a dreamer who would never amount to anything. In turn, Duke swore that he'd come back a rich and famous man someday and they'd all be sorry. But, as you well know, your grandfather died without fame."

"Or fortune," Brie added, suddenly envisioning her grandfather in a strange and different way. Drew's words had touched something deep within her. She could almost feel sorry for her grandfather. Still, to have so much pride and so little backbone that he'd turn away from his wife without even speaking to her first, simply because someone told him it was what she wanted...

"Anyway, although your grandmother never did remarry," Drew surmised, "she did go ahead with the divorce. And, according to what Duke told me, along with the final divorce papers, your grandmother had her attorney include a letter from her, stating that she was happy with her life and that she hoped he left her alone in the future. His pride undoubtedly kept him from ever going back for her. And I would suspect that on his rare visits to Georgia, it was his pride that kept him from showing that he still cared."

"My grandmother had a lot of pride, too," Brie added. Realizing that her own pride had slipped a notch and that her innermost feelings had surfaced as a result, Brie eased herself away from Drew's embrace. "Well, the point is, he shouldn't have given up so easily," she said, once again defending her original opinion of her grandfather. "And if he had truly wanted his wife and daughter with him, he wouldn't have left Georgia without them."

Drew couldn't argue that point with her because he figured she was right. If a man wanted something bad enough, he generally went after it. Drew knew he would have. In fact, just a moment ago, he'd sensed Brie's withdrawal from his arms even before she'd made a move to get away. And for just a second there, he hadn't wanted to let her go and had been tempted to tighten his hold. But he'd gotten control of himself before making that mistake. And she wasn't even his wife, for heaven's sake. She wasn't even someone he loved. *Liar.* She was just someone he'd promised to look after. She meant nothing to him, and, of course, that was why he'd been able to let her go. His pride had nothing to do with it.

But he would allow Brie to keep her pride. It was plain to see now that the other woman, the strong, prideful one, was back in control. And this was the side of Brie that didn't need anyone's help to survive.

Taking a step back, Drew lifted the lantern from the floor at his feet, turned and headed toward the doorway that led into the next room. After a moment, he glanced back and saw that Brie wasn't following him. "Well, are you coming, or not?" he asked in a gruffer voice than he intended. But he'd already admitted that he had pride, too.

Brie puckered out her bottom lip, cluing him in on the fact that his tone of voice had made a definite negative impression on her. Good. Now she knew he was back in control, too.

To Brie, the rough sound of Drew's voice demanded a prompt reply, and it took her all of a second to make up her mind. She knew from his grumpy, irritated tone that he wouldn't hesitate in leaving her behind while he looked the place over.

Therefore, she quickly decided that it was definitely in her best interest to follow along with him on his tour from room to room. After all, the only lantern she'd seen thus far was now in his possession, and while the fire in the hearth gave off some light, the lantern gave out more. And besides, the lantern was portable. When the time came, she would need it to light her way to the bathroom—which most definitely tipped the scales in favor of going along with him. She rushed to catch up.

"Watch your step," he snapped over his shoulder, bringing her to a halt several feet before she even reached him. "How many times do I have to tell you to think before you act?"

The drill sergeant was definitely back.

"At least two hundred and fifty times, sir," she retorted, wondering where the tenderhearted man from moments ago had gone. She liked that man much better than she did this guy and she wanted him back. Only, she wasn't sure why he'd left in the first place. Maybe, she decided, he simply hadn't liked comforting her as much as she had liked being comforted.

And, just in case her reasoning for the sudden change in his behavior was correct, she made sure her emotional guards were up and alert before advancing another step in his direction.

* * *

The tour was simple and quick—there wasn't much to explore. Furnishings throughout were sparse, a rickety bed and chest in one bedroom, only a small wooden desk in the other. An old refrigerator was shoved against one wall in the kitchen, and it looked as though it hadn't been used since World War II. A dust-coated metal-framed table with three matching chairs—one chair had a leg broken—crowded a tight corner next to the cabinets. If there had once been a stove in the room, it had been removed. The tour would have been extremely depressing for Brie if she hadn't decided early on to just ignore what she saw and imagine each room redecorated to her liking. And, someday, she told herself, she would see to it that they were.

"I told you there wouldn't be much to see," Drew said as they reentered the front room where the blaze in the hearth had died down to glowing embers. He tossed in several new branches and then poked at the coals beneath them until they ignited again. He stepped aside and Brie moved closer to warm herself.

Drew hated having to admit that he was worried about anyone, but he was definitely concerned about Brie. No matter what his comments had been as they'd drifted from room to room, she'd remained silent and somewhat withdrawn. Obviously, her disappointment in their findings had been too overwhelming for her to even respond. But, dammit, hadn't he tried to warn her about the condition of the place? It was in shambles.

"Look," Drew continued, "maybe coming here for the night wasn't such a good idea, after all." Let's get out of here. My apartment is a heck of a lot more comfortable than this place." He began to roll up the red sleeping bag.

"No," Brie replied quickly. She knelt next to him. "I'd really like to stay."

"But it's getting cold outside," Drew said, glancing up and finding their faces only inches apart. *Why did he always have to notice how inviting her full lips were?* Look, there's supposed to be a warming trend starting tomorrow afternoon. I don't see any reason that we should have to rough it out in the cold tonight."

"But what about security?" Brie asked, recalling the reason he'd given her for coming out here in the first place.

Dropping his eyes from her face, Drew took in a deep breath before renewing his effort to roll up the sleeping bag. "Look, Brie, I just used that as an excuse. My real reason for wanting to come out here like this was to make it as tough as possible on you—actually, I was planning to let you freeze your butt off tonight—so that by tomorrow morning you might change your mind about coming with me on the search for the treasure."

Brie couldn't believe what she was hearing. Not that she didn't honestly think that he was capable of such a devious act. Somehow, she'd known all along that he was. She just couldn't believe that she had been stupid enough to ignore that small piece of knowledge and fall for his line, anyway. How, stupid, stupid, *stupid* of her.

For once, her rising temper worked in her favor. It gave her a quick boost, and she shot to her feet. "Why, you…you…ohh…" Brie was so angry, she couldn't seem to verbalize all the terrible names she wanted to call him.

She watched as Drew rose slowly to his feet. He didn't look upset, and that angered Brie even more.

"Brie," he began, placing his hands on his hips.

And just to show him that he wasn't the leader of this cozy little twosome anymore, she did the same. To his credit, he actually gave her a moment's grin when he noticed she'd mocked him. "Brie, I know that you're upset with me. But I did it for your own good."

"Like hell you did," she retorted.

"Like hell I didn't," he argued back, but his tone wasn't nearly as threatening as when he'd yelled at her earlier to watch her step. "Look, I just want to get this all behind me—us—so that we can both get on with our lives. Don't you want the same?"

Brie lifted her chin haughtily. "Well, of course, I do."

"Then, trust me on this one issue. As inexperienced as you are, your coming with me could end up jeopardizing both our lives. With you there, I won't only have to look out for myself, but for you, too. That divides my concentration, making us both vulnerable to danger."

"But your life is already in danger. You can't do this alone."

"I can take care of myself."

"But what if you need me?"

All of Drew's breath was suddenly sucked from his body. *I do need you. No, I don't. I won't let myself. That's why I must make you stay behind.* "Brie, I've been looking out for myself for a long time now."

"I'm frightened for you."

"Don't be."

"But what if that loan shark was to suddenly decide that he's given you enough time and comes looking for you? I could help you."

"You're marrying me, remember? That's asking enough of you, already."

Then their gazes met and held like two torpedoes locked in on their targets, and it was long moments later before Drew finally spoke. "Will you think about what I just said and give me your answer in the morning?"

Suddenly Brie was experiencing an intense heat, brought on, she realized, by her awareness of Drew as the man she would always desire, no matter what. The hot, potent sensation poured over her body like rich, cream gravy, liquidizing her resolve until she simply nodded in agreement.

"Then let's get out of here," she heard Drew saying, but she was still too dazed by his nearness for her body to respond. Still gazing at him, she managed to say, "Now?"

His body came to a halt, his eyes focusing on her lips. "No—not now—at this very moment," he replied, his voice growing husky. His hand came up to the side of her face, and he gently held her there as his mouth slowly descended toward hers.

Brie's heart did a flip-flop, her eyes closed, her lips parted, and then she waited for the sweet bliss that seemed inevitable.

And, yet, it never came. In fact, it was the sudden coolness of air on her face and neck that made Brie instantly aware that Drew was no longer there. Her eyes sprang open and she saw nothing. No one. Then her gaze fell to the floor, and she saw he'd knelt and was rolling up the sleeping bags.

Had she missed something?

"What are you doing?" she heard herself asking before she could stop herself. But, finally her emotional guards kicked in with a jolt and Brie found herself wanting to melt away instead of having to deal with her own stupidity. *Oh, God, he'd never meant to kiss her. She'd just assumed he had. Well, obviously she'd missed something, all right. She'd missed what his intentions were, altogether.*

This was the second time in her life that she'd made such a ridiculous assumption. How many more times would it take before she learned her lesson?

"Never mind what I'm doing," he growled without even bothering to look at her as he rose to his full height. "Just stay put until I say it's time to go.

"Oh—and while you have the time," he said glancing back at her as he headed for the door, "think about what I asked you a moment ago." When Brie looked dumbfounded, he added, "About staying behind."

"Yeah, sure," Brie said, protecting her hurt feelings. But the truth was, she had no one to blame for them other than herself.

Hopefully, they wouldn't be in vain.

Hopefully, now that she truly understood her weakness for this man, she had learned a good and lasting lesson. One that would carry her through the next couple of days. And just for her own record keeping, she'd already made up her mind about whether she would go with him or stay behind. But she would wait and give him her answer in the morning. It would be…well…sort of her wedding gift to him. Only, he probably wasn't going to like it much.

But it didn't matter. She wasn't going to concern herself with his reaction. Because no matter what—come hell or high water—she was going along with him on that treasure hunt.

Because she knew one thing for sure. If she didn't, her future happiness would be constantly threatened by the mere fact that she had given in to her fear of loving him and turned tail instead of facing it. And after recalling the misery in her grandmother's eyes, she knew firsthand what that could do to a woman. Thanks, but no thanks. She wanted to tackle her feelings for Drew right now, while she was still young and strong enough to overcome them. Then she would get on with the rest of her life.

And only in that order.

Brie sighed deeply. If her method was such a simple solution for a woman to purge a man from her heart, she wondered why her grandmother had never thought of it....

Chapter Seven

It wasn't an alarm clock, or daybreak that drew Brie from the deep sleep that had finally claimed her in the wee hours of the morning. It was the smell of freshly brewed coffee.

Unaware that her languorous attempt to stretch out her sore, resistant muscles resembled that of a lazy, well-fed feline, Brie yawned freely. Rolling her head from one side to the other, she noticed that a small stack of logs was burning in the fireplace. The flames flickered and danced and pitched a soft, amber glow across the quiet room, which only added to her growing reluctance to rise and face the new day. Then, suddenly, remembering where she was and why she was there in the first place—*today was her wedding day, for heaven's sake*—she tossed aside the heavy blankets covering her warm body, sat up and planted her stocking feet to the floor. The pink long johns-style pajamas she'd purchased yesterday from the wilderness store hugged her slim body like a second skin. Sitting down on the sofa, she sighed, staring into the mesmerizing flames.

Almost instantly, someone tapped her shoulder from the rear. She twisted her head around to see who it was and found Drew standing just behind where she sat. He was clothed in navy jogging pants and a gray long-sleeved sweatshirt. "Good morning," he said, his voice still sounding hoarse from sleep.

"Good morning," she responded, noting that hers didn't sound much different. His, of course, was a few octaves deeper.

"Coffee?" he asked, offering her a mug, its dark, liquid contents smoking hot.

"Thanks," Brie replied, reaching for it without hesitation. She inhaled deeply, savoring the tempting aroma that drifted up. "This is what woke me up a few moments ago." Then she took her first sip and found the added taste of sugar and cream to her liking. For one fleeting moment, it occurred to her that the combination shouldn't have been just right, that Drew shouldn't have known what she liked in her coffee, but at this point it seemed rather trivial in comparison to what lay ahead of her today. Quickly, she decided she didn't care one way or the other how it had come about. By accident, or not, the blend of coffee, sugar and cream tasted great. It was just the boost she needed right then and that was all there was to it. End of discussion.

Drew walked back to the kitchen to pour himself his own dose of caffeine and returned within the minute. "Coffee's the best alarm clock I know of. Gets me up and going every time, that's for sure."

"That reminds me," Brie said, blowing at the cup of hot liquid that she held between two hands. "What time is it?"

"A little past seven. We've got to be at Jacobs's office by nine o'clock."

"I know," she said, groaning as she slowly rose from the sofa. Careful not to splatter her cup of coffee on the rug, she hobbled over to the fireplace and set the mug down on top of the mantel, purposely ignoring the two black-and-white snapshots she'd seen there the day before. She wasn't ready to stir up her emotions just yet.

Suddenly, Brie realized that she'd risen from the sofa and walked clear of it without a second thought. She was only wearing her pajamas—and nothing more! Glancing down at herself in alarm, she exhaled a quick sigh of relief when one small detail about her pj's that she'd obviously forgotten during the night hit her. Yesterday, while she and Drew were shopping for the clothing and supplies they would need for the treasure hunt, she'd taken into consideration the possibility of sharing close-quartered sleeping arrangements with him during the next several days and had chosen her sleepwear accordingly. And while her pajamas were somewhat femininely tailored—there was a cute little bow at the neckline—for them to be described as sexy or dainty or even pretty would have been an exaggeration. Frankly, the soft pink thermals covered up most of her body, with only her head, neck, hands and feet sticking out. And even her feet were covered with socks.

In her opinion, her long johns-style pajamas were nice and warm, but sexless. She saw nothing, absolutely nothing, thank the Lord, in her choice of nightwear for this occasion that could have been construed as enticing to the opposite sex. So, while she knew it certainly would have been more proper for her to have worn a robe when rising, she knew it wasn't *really* necessary. Oh, sure, she would have felt more comfortable in Drew's presence with something more than her pj's on, but, she told herself firmly once again, it wasn't *really* necessary.

Therefore, it came as a real shocker to Brie when she turned, facing Drew, and immediately noticed his slow-moving gaze strolling down the length of her body. A sudden hot flush stained her face. And when she saw his penetrating, all-male inspection traveling upward, only to have it stop and linger at her breasts, a tingling sexual awareness shuddered through her body bringing every single one of her cells to attention. It was then, as she followed the intimate direction of his eyes, that Brie suddenly realized her sexless, cover-me-up pajamas were now clinging to her erect nipples and were, indeed, most revealing. Feeling somewhat betrayed by her own body, she pretended to be suddenly chilled and, attempting to blanket herself from his view, crisscrossed her arms over her chest. Then, ever so slowly, she turned away from his probing eyes. Moments later, she glanced over her shoulder nervously and was relieved to see that he had settled back in a nearby recliner.

"You were hobbling earlier," he said matter-of-factly, stretching out his legs in front of him and crossing them at the ankles. "I warned you about the sofa. You should have listened to me and taken the bed like I offered. You would have slept a whole lot better."

"I'll be fine in a minute," Brie insisted, standing on one leg and bending the other back and forth at the knee. She was hoping to eliminate the reoccurrence of a nagging ache caused by an old injury that often gave her problems, especially when there was a sudden, rapid drop in the temperature similar to the one experienced in the area last night.

Drew took a sip of his coffee and watched her as she continued her own method of physical therapy. After a while, he said, "Old war wound?"

Turning her head to look at him, Brie frowned in confusion. When it finally occurred to her that his off-the-wall question was just his way of making idle conversation, she smiled. "Huh? Oh, no, not exactly. Actually, it was a bicycle accident that happened when I was eight years old."

"Oh? It must have been a pretty bad one. What happened?"

Remembering, Brie grimaced. "Oh, you know how kids can be sometimes. A couple of bullies dared me to ride my bike down the side of an old dried-up ravine, and like a little fool, I tried it."

"And you fell," Drew concluded.

Brie tilted her head to one side. Her face was beginning to feel flushed as a result of the heat bellowing up from the fireplace. Still, she felt she couldn't very well turn around. Not with only her Benedict Arnold pajamas on. And certainly not after the way certain parts of her body had responded earlier to his probing gaze. "Well, to be perfectly honest, that's not exactly how it happened. Actually, the sides of the ravine were deep, and I panicked when my bike started picking up too much speed. Instead of braking, I tried to jump off. Unfortunately, my shoe got caught on the pedal and I ended up landing on my right knee."

"Did you break a bone?" Drew asked, his voice genuinely concerned.

"No. But I tore up everything else. All the muscles and ligaments. My knee was a mess for a long time. Needless to say, I learned a good lesson from it all." Brie reached down and held her knee, bending her leg back and forth a couple more times.

"I bet you did." Drew smiled wryly, nodding his head in agreement. "I bet it was the last time you listened to a bully."

Thoughtful for a long moment, Brie finally said, "Well—yeah—maybe...I guess that depends on what you call a bully. But I can truthfully say that it was the very last time I ever let myself chicken out of something."

"I see," Drew said, his face slowly losing all expression. He rose from the recliner. "In other words, you're trying to tell me that you haven't changed your mind. You still plan to come with me."

"I wasn't trying to tell you any such thing. But, now that you mention it—no, I haven't changed my mind," Brie replied, a hint of challenge in her tone.

A tense silence followed. Leaning one forearm against the mantel, Brie gazed down into the fire and allowed herself to stare into the flickering flames that seemed to lick out at her.

Placing his mug next to Brie's, Drew leaned his forearm against the mantel right next to hers, emphasizing his presence at her side. "Look, we're not talking about some silly little lesson you learned back when you were eight years old, now," he said, his voice uncompromising and granite-hard.

"*I'm going,* Drew," Brie said more forcefully. Stubbornly, she kept her gaze on the fire, as though she were mesmerized. Somehow, watching the dancing flames made her feel stronger, more in control. "And that's that," she quickly added.

"Fine. That's just fine," Drew retorted, shoving himself away from the fireplace. But then he leaned down, placing his mouth close to her ear. "And what if your knee starts giving you problems and you can't keep up with me. Then what?"

"If that happens, then I guess you'll just have to leave me behind."

Drew clenched his jaw. "Exactly," he said through his teeth, moving in on her until there was barely any space between her back and his chest. It was an unnerving, almost threatening move on his part, but somehow, sensing that he would prevent her from escaping should she try, Brie didn't budge. "And if necessary, Brianna, I will do that," he taunted. "Don't make the mistake of thinking I won't. You'll only be disappointed if you do."

"If it does come to that, I'll be just fine until you come back for me," she said defiantly. "But I *am* going."

"Too chicken to 'chicken out,' is that it?"

"I'm going, Drew," she persisted, her gaze not once wavering from the flames. She knew he was trying to goad her into giving in to his wishes, but she simply wasn't going to take the bait. "And don't *you* make the mistake of thinking I'll change my mind. You'll only be disappointed if you do," she said, repeating his own words back to him.

Giving a low, drawn-out curse, Drew spun on his heels and marched up the stairs. Moments later, Brie heard when he turned on the shower in the upstairs bath. Then a door slammed shut; she took it as the only likely signal she would be given that it was time to start getting ready for their upcoming wedding. The ceremony would be taking place in less than two hours.

Suddenly, dozens of butterflies began to congregate in Brie's stomach, and during the next hour, they acted as her only indication of her true state as she flitted around from room to room, from task to task, from one thought to another. It was an effort, however, to get showered and dressed for what could have been—*should* have been—the most special, the most important occasion in her life.

Only this day meant nothing to her, nor would it ever, she told herself firmly. Repeating the vows that would make her Drew's wife wasn't a fulfillment of her dream. Drew needed her help—period. His life depended on it. Other than that, she meant nothing to him, and she wasn't going to let herself be stupid enough to believe otherwise. Not for one single moment.

But the truth was, if Brie had been completely honest with herself, she would have admitted that it didn't matter how many lectures she gave herself. Her feelings, the ones deep down inside, were either deaf, or stubborn, because they were ignoring her. According to them, where *special* and *important* were concerned, becoming Drew Naquin's wife—however temporarily—would always rank right up there at the top of their list. Always. No matter what.

On arrival at Samuel Jacobs's office, the judge signed the affidavit needed in order for Drew and Brianna to be able to waive the usual three-day waiting period. Less than ten minutes later, he pronounced them man and wife.

At this point Brie knew that most couples usually felt an enormous sense of relief wash over them and their faces radiated joy. But not this time. This time, the seconds that immediately followed the completion of the ceremony grew excessively awkward for both the bride and groom. It soon became apparent that they were at an extreme loss as to what to do with themselves now that the ceremony was actually finished.

In spite of Brie's efforts not to show her nervousness, she found herself licking her lips and clutching her hands into fists. She wished she could have whirled and, like magic, found herself someplace else. *Anyplace* else.

Suffering from a condition similar to Brie's, Drew simply wanted to escape—and he didn't care how it came about, or where he ended up. He only knew that he wanted to be gone from here. But turning away and running at this point would only prove to everyone present—including himself—that he was scared. And he had to believe he was not scared. He had to believe that he'd left that part of himself behind in his scarred childhood in one of the many foster homes he'd lived in.

Still, restlessly shifting his weight from one leg to the other, Drew couldn't deny that he was presently very uncomfortable. He glanced down at his feet and chastised himself big time for not having had the good sense to think ahead to this moment. He knew what tradition expected of him now. He was supposed to kiss the bride. But under the circumstances, he didn't know if he should—or even if he wanted to. And what if he made the expected effort and she refused him?

He tried to reassure himself. Who cared about tradition nowadays? What good would one simple little peck on the mouth do for either of them, except maybe stir up unwanted feelings? And who needed those? He sure didn't. He just wanted out of this situation—and fast.

Then again, what else could he do, with all the people from Jacobs's office standing around, watching his every move? And not only that, though he was still looking at his feet, he figured that Brie was probably watching him, too, with those big soulful eyes of hers. Not that he was about to glance in her direction to confirm his suspicions. He certainly wasn't going to give anyone, but especially not Brie, any indication of what his true emotions were. If he did, then she would have an advantage over him. And, let's face it, nobody in their right mind ever knowingly gave someone who was fast becoming a weakness for them the advantage. Damn, he wished the sick feeling inside him would just go away.

Drew inhaled deeply. Now way past the ready mark in wanting to put a stop to the clumsy awkwardness that still seemed to linger, he reached out and shook the judge's hand. "Thanks for helping us out on such short notice," he drawled. Nodding in Brie's direction, he added, "We appreciate it."

Then he pivoted on his heels and, rubbing his hands together, he said, "Okay, let's get things moving along, shall we?" He targeted Samuel Jacobs with his eyes. "You have the map, Sam?"

"Uh...yes," the attorney replied hesitantly, obviously ruffled by Drew's sudden briskness.

"Could you hand it over now? I really need to be on my way. Time's running short."

Jacobs shrugged. "Why would you say that? You've already made the only deadline that Duke stipulated in his will."

"But I have my own deadline," Drew remarked. "And my own reasons for it."

"Well, certainly Miss Stansbury has some say in this matter."

Drew frowned at the attorney. "She's had a recent name change, Sam."

"Uh...right," Jacobs replied, tossing a glance in Brie's direction. "Pardon me—*Mrs. Naquin*."

Without looking directly at Drew—actually, Drew suddenly realized that Brie hadn't really looked directly at him since they'd left his apartment this morning—she spoke up for the first time. "I appreciate your concern on my behalf, Mr. Jacobs. But Drew's reasons for wanting to get this ordeal behind us are valid ones. And he's right. There's no time to waste. Please, give us the map so we can be on our way."

Drew gave Brie a determined glare. "I don't care what you say, you're *not* coming with me."

"I am," she replied, jutting out her chin stubbornly.

"I've made up my mind, Brianna. It's too dangerous. *You're not coming.*"

Brie turned to Samuel Jacobs. "What happens if one of us isn't permitted by the other to participate in the treasure hunt? In a sense, wouldn't that make my grandfather's will null and void? And, instead of giving us the map, wouldn't you have to destroy it, instead?"

"Um…well…" Jacobs became flushed. "I…uh…I don't know. I mean, I suppose so," he stammered. "I'd have to give the matter some serious consideration before drawing a final conclusion."

Drew stepped forward, his face impassive. "Well, you take your time doing just that, Samuel, while I speak to my *wife* in private." Angrily, he stormed up to Brie, grabbed her by the arm and insisted she accompany him to an area away from prying ears. The small secluded library in the next room served the purpose he had in mind. He pulled Brie inside after him and closed the door. "Now, listen here," he said, turning her to face him. "If you don't shut up, you're going to screw up everything."

"For who? You?"

"And you, too."

"I don't believe that for a minute."

"Look, I'm going to level with you. The deal about the loan shark—"

"Was a lie," Brie cut in, finishing his sentence for him.

Drew's mouth dropped open in surprise. "How did you know?"

Brie smiled smugly. "I'm dense and a little slow, but eventually, even *I* figure things out. It helped, of course, when I overheard your conversation on the telephone with someone by the name of Thompson."

"Thompson?" he repeated, an incredulous expression seizing hold of his face. "You were listening in when he called this morning?"

"Not intentionally. I'd just finished blow-drying my hair in the downstairs bath and I saw that you hadn't come down to leave yet, so I picked up the phone in the kitchen to make a call, heard your voice mention my name and listened for a moment. Just long enough, in fact, to hear you telling your old buddy this laughable story about how you lied to Duke's poor granddaughter so that you could get your hands on some treasure map."

Drew's face grew solemn. "Look, you don't understand. You don't know the whole story."

"Oh, I just bet I don't. Especially if it was left up to you to tell me," Brie taunted. Since hearing his devious little confession over the telephone, she'd done her best to control her rising temper. She'd restrained her fiery reaction because she'd known that she needed to keep a cool, clear head. She'd had a decision to make rather quickly. But maybe now it was time she let Drew know just how upset she really was with him.

Still, she wanted to be careful of what she told him. She never, ever wanted him to know how vulnerable she'd felt inside, or how hurt she'd been to discover his deception... or how foolish she'd been for trusting him.

She straightened her shoulders. "So what were you planning to do once the treasure was found? Take it and then just disappear?"

He glared at her. "No, not exactly. I'd always planned to give you your share."

"Really?" Brie asked sarcastically. "And I suppose you expect me to believe that?"

Placing his hands on his hips and staring at a distant point over her shoulder, Drew's lips tightened into a narrow line. Finally he replied, "No, I guess not." Then he turned his gaze back to her face. "Seems you're calling the shots now. So, what are you going to do?"

Brie took a deep, steadying breath. She had waited for this moment, when she would be in control and he would be at her mercy, but now that the moment had arrived, she found herself disappointed. She disliked anyone who tried to control others. She much preferred getting a person's attention because they wanted to give it to her, not because she had an advantage over them. And, of course, that was a two-way street. She didn't like being manipulated by others, either. Still, it probably wouldn't hurt anything if she were the controlling factor in this little game. After all, this entire situation wasn't any of her doing in the first place.

She frowned. "I feel I should go back in there and tell Mr. Jacobs to just destroy the map."

"Then go ahead," Drew drawled, his features drawn. "I won't stop you."

Brie hated the weakness within that yearned to reach out to him. *He had lied to her, for heaven's sake. Why was she still so tempted to place her destiny in his manipulative hands?*

"But, then again," she said, making a split-second decision, one she hoped she wouldn't live to regret, "I've come this far, why quit now?" She smiled cynically. "However, if we continue with this treasure hunt," she added, pausing to look directly into his eyes, "I feel you should know that I've changed my mind about something."

The only response Drew gave was to lift his dark eyebrows in question.

"I want my share."

One corner of Drew's mouth hinted at a smile. He looked almost amused. "Sure. I wouldn't dream of having it any other way."

"And I'm going with you. In fact," Brie said, taking a deep breath and licking her lips, "I'm going to be perfectly honest, it's the only way I feel I can trust you now."

Once again, Drew's glance moved from hers. A muscle twitched in his jaw. When he finally returned his gaze to her, his features were stiff. "Who will be giving the orders while we're out there searching for the bounty?"

"Nothing's changed with that—you have the experience. Therefore, you will, of course."

"And will you promise to follow every order I give you?"

Brie started to nod but stopped when he quickly added the words, "No matter what I tell you to do?"

Hesitating, she searched his face for some kind of warning that would prove to her she would be crazy to give him her word on such an agreement. But she saw nothing sinister in the steady gaze he returned. "Yes, I promise," she finally answered.

"Okay, then," Drew replied. "You and I have a deal. If either of us breaks it, the game's over."

"All right," Brianna said, taking a step toward the door. But Drew quickly blocked her path. "Not so fast. I have another question for you."

She looked up in surprise. "Now what?"

"You had plenty of time to get out of this mess before letting it go this far. So why didn't you?"

Brie shrugged. "I guess my curiosity has gotten the better of me. This morning, after realizing your life wasn't really in any kind of danger, I figured that if going after Old Gabe's treasure was worth that much trouble to you, then maybe it was worth my time, as well. So, after making that decision, there was only one thing left for me to do—and that was to go through with the marriage so we could get our hands on the map." Completing that statement, she sidestepped around Drew, then stopped and looked back over her shoulder. "But then again, maybe I just felt like getting even. Now we both know how it feels to be duped by the other." Reaching the door, she opened it and walked back into Samuel Jacobs's office, where everyone was still waiting for them.

"Brie?" Drew called after her. Once again, she halted and glanced back. "You know, there just might be another reason why you didn't back out."

Brie's insides froze in place as she waited for him to continue.

Drew developed a wide, cocky-looking grin. "Maybe the idea of going after a buried treasure has awakened a whole new set of genes inside you that you've been able to overlook until now. Maybe there's more of old Duke in you than you care to admit."

Brie glared at him. "And maybe you've simply lost your mind," she snapped testily.

His grin spread wider. "Well, ma'am," he said in an exaggerated drawl, "I guess we'll just have to wait and see about that, now, won't we?"

Once more Drew and Brie were alone in the library. Only this time, the main focus of their attention was on the map that Drew had pulled from the manila folder given to him moments ago. After carefully unfolding the white piece of paper, he spread the drawing out on the long table in front of him without uttering a single comment.

Brie kept her eyes on his face for a moment before lowering them to examine the map for herself. Silently, she peered down at the drawing, and, within a short span of time, came to a shocking conclusion of her own.

True, she was an amateur when it came to reading old treasure maps, having literally no experience whatsoever in that field. But, in her opinion, if indeed that white piece of paper on the table was the authentic map to Old Gabe's treasure, then something was terribly wrong. The paper wasn't even old-looking—certainly not as old-looking as she'd expected it to be. It wasn't yellow, or stained, or even tattered along the edges. It wasn't even drawn on century-old parchment paper, as she had assumed it would be. Instead, the "like-new" map had been hand-etched in dark lead on a plain white sheet of paper that looked as though its perforated sides had been removed. *Like computer paper.* Why, that alone dated the map to modern times. But even if she was wrong about the perforated sides, could any single piece of paper survive two hundred years without some evidence of aging? Hardly.

Brie took a step back, trying to put together all the pieces in her mind. She still hadn't come to terms with herself as to why, after learning about Drew's deception, she'd gone ahead with the demands of her grandfather's will. Maybe the excuse she had given Drew was true. Maybe she *had* somehow convinced herself that she deserved her share of the bounty. But whether it was her motive for going ahead and marrying him—she certainly wasn't going to consider the possibility that it might be something more, as in her feelings for him—as far as he and the world were concerned, it was as good an alibi as any. She was sticking to it, no matter what.

Brie took a deep breath. "Okay, Drew, I think it's time you level with me. Is this, or is this not, the map to Old Gabe's treasure?"

It took him several long seconds to finally lift his head and look at her. "Huh? Oh—no, it isn't."

Her breath locked in her throat. "You mean it's a fake?"

Drew nodded. "Yeah. And a bad one at that."

"Oh, God," Brie exclaimed. "Do you mean to say that we've gotten married for nothing?"

"No, I didn't say that. I said this wasn't a map to Old Gabe's treasure, and it isn't. But it *is* a treasure map. I'm just not sure to what."

"Do you suppose my grandfather knew it was a fake?"

"I would suppose so. In fact, I think he's the one who drew it up."

"What? But why?"

Drew shrugged. "I don't know. Maybe something happened to the original, or maybe he only got a glimpse of something he thought was Old Gabe's treasure and drew this map from memory."

"Oh, God. Then it's worthless, isn't it?"

Drew shook his head. "No, not necessarily."

Paling, Brie felt as though her insides were going to explode. "So, everything we've done so far has been for nothing. All my grandfather wanted to do was take us on one big ride. His way of having a last big adventure." Brie's voice caught in her throat. "How could he do that?"

Drew grabbed Brie by the shoulders. "Hey, look, we've already come this far, I say let's go for it." He shrugged to emphasize his point. "What do we have to lose?"

Brie looked up at him, her heart throbbing against her chest. "Nothing, I guess."

"That's right," he said, an undercurrent of excitement in his voice. "And we've got everything to gain." Suddenly, with their faces only inches apart, his intense, hungry gaze dropped to her lips and Brie felt as though she were going to be eaten alive.

His hand cupped the side of her face and his gaze grew increasingly warmer until it was hot and sensual and potent with desire. Then his lips parted slightly, and his head lowered toward hers. "I think I was supposed to kiss my bride earlier," he said huskily, his mouth covering hers.

Within moments all of Brie's emotional guards, the ones she'd trained so well, had turned tail and run away, leaving her vulnerable and alone to fight against her own flourishing desires. She wanted to pull away, yet she didn't. She wanted to hate the mesmerizing control he held over her, yet she couldn't. She had lost the battle—and he had won. Giving in to his kiss, she realized she was giving in to much more. There was no hiding or denying it from herself any longer. She was in love with Drew Naquin, and she would forever love him, in spite of the fact that she knew she could never compete with the only true love of his life—adventure. Her feelings for him would have to remain her own little secret. And with that in mind, she quickly gathered up enough courage to pull away from him.

Drew didn't resist her efforts to end the moment. Instead, his attention immediately returned to the map on the table. He picked it up, folded it into quarters and slipped it back into the manila folder. Then, pretending as if nothing at all had just transpired between them, he looked at her, smiled and said, "Let's get going."

Just like that. Wham—*let's get going*. No *I'm sorry, I shouldn't have kissed you*. No nothing. "Where are we heading?" she asked lightly, her heart pounding in her chest.

"The Atchafalaya Basin—just like I thought."

Brie swallowed down her reaction to him and told herself to get tough. "So, you do understand the directions on the map?"

"Yeah," he drawled, opening the door and stepping aside so she could exit the library first. "And with any luck, we just might have it by tonight."

Looking back at him, Brie's eyes widened. "Are you kidding me?"

He smiled at her enthusiasm. "Nope. I'm not kidding."

"Then I could be on my way back to Georgia as early as tomorrow," she said, wondering why her heart suddenly felt so heavy.

Attempting another grin, one corner of Drew's mouth lifted. "Yeah, how about that?" he said, trying hard to ignore the fact that there wasn't a single ounce of joy to be found in him at the thought of her leaving. When had he come to think of her as a necessary part of his future happiness?

"By the way," he said as they walked out of the attorney's office and into the bright midmorning sunshine, "I've been meaning to ask you something for a while."

"What's that?"

His eyebrows furrowed. "Who were you going to telephone this morning when you picked up on my conversation with Thompson? Are you really getting that lonesome for your boyfriend?"

Chapter Eight

The farce had gone on long enough, Brie decided. It was time to end the misunderstanding concerning her personal life. She was ready to come clean. Therefore, without so much as turning her head in Drew's direction, she hurried down the sidewalk leading from the law office and headed toward his pickup truck. The entire time, she was very much aware that Drew was following close at her heels. Finally, she glanced over her shoulder at him and said, "I don't have a boyfriend, Drew."

"Well, excuse me," he replied sarcastically. "Actually, the word I should have used was fiancé."

Frustrated with him—with herself, with everything—Brie reached the pickup, yanked open the passenger door and climbed inside in what looked like one fluid movement. By the time she'd settled in, Drew had already situated himself so that it was impossible for her to shut the door. His blocking stance reeked of pure male arrogance. From that ploy alone, as well as from the smirk lurking at the corners of his mouth, Brie knew he was waiting for her to say something, anything, in answer to his last remark. Folding her arms across her chest, she gazed at him. "I don't have a fiancé, either."

"You don't?" he repeated, and for a second he looked as though the news had startled him. But then he came back with that same smirk he'd had on his face earlier. "Then who were you trying to call?"

"That, Drew Naquin, is none of your business. Now, will you please move so I can shut my door?"

He started to step away but then stopped and grimaced at her. "Wait just one darn minute here. What do you mean, you don't have a fiancé?"

Brie shrugged. "Look, I'm sorry to disappoint you, but I don't have one, okay?"

"You do."

"I don't."

"You don't?"

"No—I don't."

Drew's hands went to his hips. His eyes narrowed. "But you said—"

"I didn't say any such thing," Brie confessed. "You were the one who assumed I was engaged. Remember yesterday when we were at the courthouse getting the marriage license? You were the one who brought up the subject."

"Well, you certainly didn't deny anything."

"I didn't feel it was necessary for me to have to defend myself. To begin with, what difference should it make to you if I'm engaged, or not, to someone else?"

"Well—none," Drew lied roughly, knowing full well that it *did* make a big difference, to him, to everything. If what she said was true—*and let's face it, why would she lie*—then Duke's will . . . their marriage . . . it had all been for nothing.

Only now it was too late to do things differently. Duke was gone and his will would forever stand as written. And right along with that unchanging fact went another one— Brie's inheritance still needed to be found before she discovered it existed and targeted him as the prime suspect in its disappearance. Especially now that she knew he'd lied to her once already. So, in reality, she was right. Whether she was engaged no longer made a difference. He was still in dire straits to find her money.

Shrugging, Drew gave her a slight grin. "I just thought you were engaged to be married, that's all."

"I was, but I broke it off a couple of weeks ago, okay? Now, could we drop the subject please?" Brie asked.

"Yeah—sure—consider it done," he replied, slamming shut the passenger door and then strolling around the front of his pickup to get in on the driver's side. She'd said that she was the one who had broken off her engagement, right? Well, looky here, but wasn't that a kick in the rear? Because, right alongside that little enlightenment came a more unsettling one. His promise to Duke had been for nothing, after all. Obviously Miss Brianna Stansbury—uh, Mrs. Drew Naquin, was quite capable of taking care of herself.

Yeah, but get off your soapbox, will you? his inner voice chimed in. *You know, and I know, that you wouldn't have missed spending this time with Brie for anything. Simply 'cause you know this is it. This is all you're gonna ever have. These are your memories for the future. For when the thrill of adventure has gone away and your nights get long and lonely. True, you're being a hard mule, but it's only to keep her at bay. Actually, you're loving every minute of being in her company. It's an adventure you'll*

play over and over in your mind forever. And you know in
your heart it'll never grow old—not like all the others will.
So, go on. Be a man. Admit it. You wouldn't have missed
this for the world.

Yeah, well, he was thrilled, all right, Drew told himself,
but not for the reasons his consciousness would have liked
him to believe. Sure, he was damned glad to learn that she
had gotten rid of that scumbag swindler she'd been engaged to. But that was simply because he liked—*not*
loved—her and thought she deserved better.

And, just for the record, he wanted it to be known
throughout his body and soul that he didn't love anybody. Nor did he want to. And that was all there was to it.

To his way of thinking, that straightforward statement
was more than enough to settle any doubts his inner self
might have had concerning who he really was and what
really made him tick.

But, much to his growing disappointment, even after his
little speech to himself, Drew still sensed a nagging doubt
running loose somewhere inside. A nagging little doubt
indicating that, in spite of himself, he'd fallen in love with
Brie, anyway.

Drew drove his pickup away from Lafayette and headed
east on Interstate 10. Brie sat silently on the passenger side
and studied the like-new treasure map that she'd taken the
liberty of removing from the manila folder Samuel had
placed it in. She turned the map this way, and then that
way, but nothing seemed to help. She simply couldn't make
heads or tails of the directions.

Noticing her confusion, Drew reached over and turned
the map completely around. "This is north," he said.

"Oh," Brie replied.

"Right now, we're heading east."

"I see."

Using his finger, Drew traced the path they would be taking. "We're going to turn south here. Then we'll head east again, then south once more." He thumped the paper with the tip of his finger. "The treasure is buried right about here. See the small X your grandfather made?"

"I see," Brie said, but, of course, she really didn't. Unless that tiny little mark was it. Good grief, she almost needed a magnifying glass to see it. Soon after, she folded the map in quarters and placed it back in the manila folder on the seat between them.

Finally, Drew veered off Interstate 10. He headed for the small fishing village that jutted up against the levee surrounding Lake Henderson. From this particular point, Drew knew he had access to various destinations within the Atchafalaya Basin.

He followed the main road through town, crossing the small bridge over Bayou Amy, and then slowly climbed the high wall of dirt surrounding Lake Henderson. Here Brie got her first glimpse of the clear, dark water of the Atchafalaya Basin. But then Drew aimed his pickup down a rutted dirt path that carved its way along the back side of the grass-covered levee and her view of the lake was immediately blocked by the tall mound weaving its way ahead of them in the distance like a huge green serpent.

Finally they came to a handmade sign with a red arrow pointing directly over the levee. It read: Boat Landing. Maneuvering the vehicle over the levee at the speed of a slow-climbing roller coaster, Drew drove into a graveled lot and parked his truck next to several other pickup trucks, that had empty boat trailers hooked to their bumpers.

"Coming?" Drew asked, opening his door and jumping out.

Brie climbed out a few seconds after him and walked to where he stood, facing the lake. And then for a while, they both stared out over the open water.

Brie decided that she agreed with the colorful travel brochures displayed in all of the tourist shops along Interstate 10. They testified to the fact that the Atchafalaya Basin was an area of unspoiled beauty—Mother Nature at her finest. So far, she'd seen only a small part—a very civilized part, at that—but she had to admit it was awesome. As far as she could see in the distance, Lake Henderson was filled with hundreds, probably thousands of cypress trees. Most were stumps, some just barely topping the water, while others lay just beneath its surface. Obviously, certain areas of the lake were treacherous for boating. But also quite obvious was the fact that the Cajun people who had settled in this region knew the secrets of their swamp and were able to capitalize on its many natural resources, such as seafood from its lakes and bayous, and oil and gas from beneath its rich soil.

But even with all of their beauty, swamps were scary places, too. At least, for Brie they were. She saw them as dark, damp, low sections of land where green fungus grew on everything. In her opinion, all things that lived in a swamp were slimy and had a way of slithering by, instead of walking. Simply put, swamps gave her the creeps.

"Here," Drew said, pulling her from her daze by offering her a clear plastic bottle filled with some kind of yellowish concoction. He'd obviously retrieved it from his truck while she'd been lost in thoughts of creepy-crawly things. "Spray this on any exposed flesh. It'll keep the mosquitoes away."

"How did you know I was thinking along those lines?"

"I could tell by the expression on your face."

She looked at him blankly.

"You looked ready to jump back in the truck and make a mad dash back to Interstate 10 before something got the chance to jump out of the water and grab you."

Brie gave a half smile. "You're right. I think I was letting my thoughts run away with me." Then she gazed down at the bottle he'd given her and frowned. She didn't like the idea of using chemicals on her skin. And this bottle didn't even have a label. "What is this?"

Drew shrugged. "It's a combination of bath oil and water. It's safe to use as an insect repellent and it works."

Brie swatted at a mosquito and missed. Within a second, it was back and she swung at it again, and missed. Oh, what the heck, she told herself. If she didn't do something now to discourage these damned mosquitoes, she was going to look like an overgrown kid with acne all over her body. Home remedy or not, she was using it. Besides, how harmful were a few chemicals, anyway? Undoubtedly, once she entered the swamp, the mosquito repellent she wore on her skin would be the least of her worries. She would probably be darn lucky if she didn't catch malaria, or worse.

Squirting a generous amount in the palm of her hand, Brie rubbed the oil-based concoction into her skin. She looked around for Drew and saw he'd already walked away and was talking to a toothless old man in scraggly-looking khaki clothes. The man's brown skin looked leathered from either age, or from too many years under a hot, penetrating sun. She overheard when the old man said in a scratchy Cajun accent that he'd spent the entire morning on the levee, "fishin' fer gar." She watched as Drew nodded his head in what looked to be complete understanding of that statement. Brie, however, had no earthly idea what *gar* was. Undoubtedly, it lived in water—but then, so did the monster from the Black Lagoon. But nobody ever fished for him.

Then Drew asked the old-timer if he could recall the last time he'd seen her grandfather. That question did away with Brie's silly thoughts on monsters that lived beneath the water and grabbed hold of her immediate, undivided attention. She stepped a few feet closer to them, waiting for the Cajun to answer Drew's inquiry.

"Let's see," the old man said, scratching the back of his balding head. "I ges it was near three weeks ago—maybe a month."

"Was he alone?"

"Yep," he said. "I kin recall that real good. He was alone." The toothless old man turned and pointed to a paint-free, weather-worn building along the bank that had a sign over the entrance door reading, Tee Boy's Bait Stand. Right beneath it someone had added in red paint *and Boat Landing*. "He asked to borrow Tee Boy's boat and then went out all by hisself. Yep, I kin recall that real good."

"Which way did he go?" Drew asked.

The man turned sideways and, with a finger crippled with arthritis, pointed toward the southeast. "Ahtta way."

"And he came back alone?"

"Yep."

"How long would you say he was gone?"

"Well, let's see..." The old man was scratching his head again. "I was gittin' ready to go fishin' when I saw him leavin' the first time, and it was dark when he come back."

"You mean he stayed gone all day, from early morning until sometime after dark that night?"

"Yep. That's what I'm sayin'. Tee Boy was all mad about it, too. He thought old Duke had done gone and turned his boat over in the basin." Then, after giving his story some additional thought, the old Cajun nodded his head. "Yep. I kin recall that day real good."

Drew listened intently to every answer given him by the Cajun before asking the next one. "When you saw Duke leaving that morning, did you happen to notice if he had any supplies in the boat with him? Or perhaps, something that might have looked unusual? Like maybe a small chest?"

The old man thought for a moment. "Nope. I don't recall seein' nothin' unusual. Why you askin' me that?"

Yeah, Brie wondered. Why was he asking that? Considering the circumstances, she thought it rather an odd question, too.

"No reason," Drew answered. "Just curious."

"Yep," the aging fisherman said, slowly shaking his head as he turned to walk away, "I'm sure gonna miss old Duke. Me and him liked to talk on occasion. And he sure liked the way I cooked them garfish. It just ain't gonna be the same without him comin' around no more."

Suddenly tears dampened Brie's eyes. *Her grandfather really was gone, wasn't he?* Sometimes the reality of it was simply too much.

Having heard enough of their conversation, Brie turned away and walked hastily down the boat dock.

As strange as it seemed, she suddenly felt somewhat frightened, as though her grandfather's passing had made her alone in the world. And in reality, it had. She was the only one left in her family. Yet the feeling really didn't make any sense, considering that she'd hardly ever even seen her grandfather over the years, much less depended on him for any kind of emotional support. Nonetheless, she had to rub her upper arms to brush away a chill of uncertainty that wanted to seize hold of her. Because in that particular moment, there was no denying that she missed him as much as she had ever missed anyone. Then again, because of the many regrets in their relationship and the knowledge that time had finally run out for them to make changes for the better, she probably missed her grandfather more.

The cold snap from the night before had long ago disappeared and the midday sun had temperatures warming into the low sixties. Looking north, Brie knew from Drew's earlier explanation that the interstate highway from which they'd exited was just beyond her sight, carrying traffic east and west across the state of Louisiana. Built just over twenty years ago, it was the first real form of modern civilization to successfully penetrate its way through the Atchafalaya Basin, which had, up until that time, remained virtually a wilderness. To the east was Baton Rouge and to her west was Lafayette. To the north, as well as to the south, was swampland. But then, down below the swamp, splashing up against the sandy Louisiana coastline, lay the beautiful Gulf of Mexico.

"Ready?" Drew asked, making her aware of his presence nearby.

Startled, Brie whirled. "Now where are we going?"

"A few miles down the levee," he said, pointing in that direction.

"And then where?" she asked.

Drew sighed. "Look, considering that you won't even know when we get there, let's just take one step at a time, okay?"

"In other words, trust you."

"Exactly," Drew replied.

"Do I have a choice?"

"Yes, as a matter of fact, you do. I can bring you back to Lafayette and put you on the next flight back to Atlanta."

"But then I'd have to trust that you'd call me the minute you found something, right?"

"You'd have my word on it."

Brie looked him steady in the eye. "I'm almost tempted," she said. "To believe you, that is. But not to return to Atlanta."

The corners of Drew's mouth hinted at a smile. "Well, that's a start, anyway. For a while, I didn't think you believed in me, period."

"For a while, I didn't," Brie added with spunk. Then she shrugged. "And who knows? Later on I might be sorry that I did this time. But for now, I'm going on intuition."

His grin grew sexy—no, more cocky— No, she'd been right the first time. It grew sexy. "Then I guess I'll have to make it a point not to disappoint you, my dear Mrs. Naquin," he drawled playfully, sweeping his agile body into an exaggerated bow.

The emphasis he'd placed on her new name shook Brie. Marrying him was one thing. But having him refer to her by his own surname was something else entirely. It didn't sound right. Not that it sounded wrong. It just sounded...well...different. She wasn't accustomed to it. *Mrs. Drew Naquin. Mrs. Brie Naquin. Brie Naquin.*

Brie tilted her head as she considered the sound of it. Well...maybe she'd been mistaken, after all. Because now that she'd rehearsed the name change over and over in her mind, it did seem to have a certain ring to it that was sort of—well—majestic.

She glanced over at Drew and found the most unusual, melancholy look on his face. "What's the matter?" she asked.

Drew shook his head. "Nothing, really. It's just that sometimes . . . well, a certain expression you have reminds me of Duke, and it always takes me by surprise when it does.''

Brie smiled sadly. ''You really do miss him, don't you?''

''Yeah, I really do,'' Drew said, tucking his hands into the front pockets of his jeans. He turned and headed toward the truck. Brie fell in step beside him.

But just before climbing aboard, she glanced back at the clear dark water of Lake Henderson and smiled again. And as a warm feeling slowly oozed over her, she realized that Drew had just given her a compliment that she knew would grow more touching to her heart with each passing day.

She glanced over at him, and he turned and smiled. And for that moment, she felt at peace with herself.

Finally Drew stopped the truck, parked and killed the engine. But it wasn't until he jumped out and began to unload their supplies that Brie realized they'd reached yet another stage in their journey to find the treasure. She watched as he carried their two bedrolls to a single metal boat that was docked at the bank. Then he came back and began to reorganize their boxes of supplies, explaining to Brie that he thought the treasure would take them only a few hours to find, and, therefore, it was unnecessary for them to bring along all the items he'd brought from his apartment. However, he made sure their shovels were included in the supplies he did plan to take.

Brie was leery of getting into the narrow, low-sided boat and watched carefully as Drew got in and made his way to the back. It rocked sideways under his moving weight. Balancing himself quite easily, he turned and faced Brie. ''Untie the rope,'' he commanded. Brie hurriedly did as he bid and then looked up, waiting for her next instructions.

"Okay, now shove off and then hop in—fast," he ordered.

Brie remembered that she'd promised to follow all of his commands. She figured that included even the ones she wasn't sure of. Therefore, without further ado, she bent over, gave the front of the boat a big push and, much to her surprise, sent it gliding away from the bank. Surprised to have succeeded on her first attempt, she watched as it drifted farther out.

"Brie—hurry up—get in!" Drew bellowed, causing her to jerk to attention. Realizing in that split second that the boat was already several feet away, she made a wild dive for it.

Luckily, she made it, landing on her stomach, her arms and legs sprawled out in all directions, amid wooden paddles, orange-colored life jackets, seat cushions, bright-colored bedrolls—and a tackle box that turned over, spilling hooks and lures.

"Dammit, Brie, why did you wait so long?" she heard Drew ask as he stepped over a sleeping bag, a paddle and both life jackets to reach her. Grabbing hold of her shoulders, he helped her gather herself up in one piece—thank heaven. He held on to her until she was steady enough to sit down. "Are you all right?"

"Yes," Brie said, rubbing at a burning pain in one shoulder. Apparently, she'd struck it against the boat when she'd landed. But, other than that, she was okay. "I think either the blue bedroll or one of the seat cushions must have saved me from breaking any bones."

Drew released a heavy sigh of relief. "Thank goodness." Then, checking her over, he asked, "Are you hurting anywhere?"

"My shoulder," Brie said, grimacing. "I must have bruised it."

Drew immediately began to massage her injured shoulder, gently working his fingers into the muscle to soothe the burning ache. "Does this help?"

"Uh-huh," she replied, closing her eyes.

"Look, I'm really sorry about this."

"Forget it. It's my own fault. I shouldn't have let the boat drift off so far before jumping in."

"No, it's my fault. I knew your lack of experience. I should have realized that something like this could happen."

"Look," Brie said, "like I've told you already... I'm a tough cookie."

Drew gave her a lopsided grin. "Yeah—you sure are."

Then for the longest time, they just grinned at each other.

Finally, Drew said, "Feel better now?"

"Mmm... much," she replied without looking up at him. "Thanks."

"Don't mention it," he said. After several moments, his fingers relaxed and the magical feeling they had given Brie immediately subsided. A second later she opened her eyes to discover him presenting her with one of the orange life jackets. "It's time we get started. Here, put this on."

Soon they were on their way, riding over the calm, clear waters of the Atchafalaya Basin for what seemed like hours and hours. In reality, it was less than forty-five minutes.

But Brie was in a predicament. One that would require her having some privacy in order to alleviate the problem. It didn't have to be much of a place. Just a simple little nook that would hide her away from any possible observers. And it would only take a couple of minutes. Maybe three at the most.

Still, she doubted Drew's understanding in the matter. Men never seemed to understand.

Therefore, knowing the annoyed reaction of most men to the request she was going to make of Drew, she took a deep breath and then glanced back at him. "How much farther?" she shouted over the noise of the outboard motor.

Drew shook his head. "Not much. Why?" he asked, his eyes narrowed against the wind whipping across his face.

Brie swallowed. "I know I should have taken care of this matter before we got in the boat, but it wasn't a necessity at the time. But now it's become urgent."

"What matter?" he shouted back at her.

She could tell he didn't have any idea what she was talking about. "I—I need some privacy, Drew."

"Privacy? What kind of privacy?"

Not wanting to go into any more detail than necessary, Brie reached inside of her purse, pulled out a pocket-size box of tissue paper and held it up for him to see. "I need to go," she said, mouthing the words so that he could read her lips rather than hear her.

"Oh, good grief," he said. "Already?"

She had known he would react this way.

But even though Brie had prepared herself for his reaction, she was still disappointed that he wasn't more understanding. This wasn't her fault, for heaven's sake. She didn't have control over this kind of situation any more than she did over the amount of oxygen she required to live. It was a bodily function. Human. Automatic. Men needed to realize that.

Brie was tempted to snap back at him, but then decided that it wouldn't be in her best interest. So, instead, she gave him a beguiling smile. "Could you please pull up to that little island straight ahead?"

"You mean Snake Island?"

Brie's eyes widened as she looked toward the land mass she'd pointed out to him and then glanced back. *"Snake Island?"*

Slowing down the motor, Drew nodded. "Uh-huh. That's not its actual name, but that's what I call it. 'Cause every time I come out here during the summer months, there's always a lot of snakes coiled up, sunning themselves on the bank. And to tell you the truth, it hasn't been that cold down here this fall, so they're probably still around—somewhere."

Brie shivered at the thought of going ashore and meeting up with a coiled snake. Thanks, but no thanks. She could keep herself on hold for a while longer. Not much longer, but enough to make it to another island. "Never mind. I think I can wait," she replied.

Drew pointed ahead. "I know a better place. It's just around that bend. Can you make it that far?"

"Yes," Brie shouted back, now certain that she could. Having turned sideways in her seat in order to hear Drew when he spoke, she now faced herself to the front. The noisy outboard motor pushed the small boat forward, plowing a path through the water straight ahead.

Just before they reached the bend, Brie glanced to her right and saw a heavyset man with a long, mossy-looking beard standing in an old wooden boat that had been driven up to the bank. He wore a pair of old dungarees, caked with mud from his knees on down. Since Brie hadn't seen another living thing other than several long-legged birds that Drew called egrets and one small alligator, the simple discovery of another living soul way out here beyond civilization wasn't meant to be taken lightly. She sat up straight and waved at him.

Drew leaned forward and shouted out for her benefit, "He's trapping."

"What do you mean?" Brie asked, keeping her eyes pinned toward the bank.

"He sets traps to capture animals for their fur."

Looking back at Drew, Brie grimaced. "Isn't that illegal?"

"Not for certain animals. And not at certain times of the year. This man's family has probably always lived back here in these swamps. Most likely, his father was a trapper. And probably so was his grandfather and great-grandfather. It's all he's ever known."

Brie found herself nodding in understanding. In fact, she now felt she knew exactly what it was like to want to carry on one's family heritage—no matter what that heritage might be, or how it was perceived by others. And while she didn't particularly like his trade, she really did feel she understood where the trapper was coming from. He had inherited a way of life that was a means of survival for him.

Soon they had rounded the bend and Drew was aiming their boat toward a narrow strip of land that extended from the mainland. It was higher in elevation than the others within their viewing distance. Ordering Brie to remain seated until he told her otherwise, Drew killed the outboard motor, climbed over the supplies that were in his way to get to the front and then waited for the boat to come near enough to the bank so that he could hop out. "Throw me the rope," he commanded the moment his feet hit solid ground.

Brie quickly tossed the rope at him, and he grabbed hold of it and dragged the front end of the boat onshore. Then he tied the rope around the small trunk of a nearby willow tree. "Come on," he said, offering Brie his outstretched hand and steadying her as she stepped from the boat. This time she made it without mishap.

"Thank you," she said.

Her hand was still nestled in Drew's and he gave no indication that he intended on letting go of her any time soon. "Let's check out this area," he said, pulling her along with him.

She liked the way he'd said that. As though they really were in this together. Even if they were only looking for a place of privacy for her.

Drew scanned the area carefully, using his feet to stomp down tall weeds and briars. Within moments, he'd made a small clearing for her, secluded from anyone's view. "I think you'll be safe here," he said, dropping her hand and turning to walk away. "If you need me, call. I'll be right over here, okay?"

"Okay," she replied with a tentative smile. She knew she was safe—she felt safe—but still her heart was pounding. She hoped he didn't walk away too far and would have told him as much if she hadn't decided it would make her sound like a big baby.

She had just finished and was coming out from the clearing to meet Drew when she heard something—a voice, maybe—in the distance. Then she heard it again, and this time she was certain it was a voice—faint—calling for help. She stopped, listened and heard it again. A fearful, almost smothering feeling swelled inside of her; and, with her heart hammering in her ears, she broke into a run. "Drew," she yelled out, flying forward.

Suddenly, from out of nowhere, it seemed, he was there and she flung herself into his arms. "Oh, God," she said breathlessly. "I thought something had happened to you."

"The same here," Drew said, crushing her body against his. He was as breathless as she was. If something had happened to her, God, he would have died on the inside. "Are you all right? I thought I heard you calling for help."

"It wasn't me," she replied. "But I did hear someone."

"Me, too," he said, loosening his embrace. They both grew quiet and listened.

A second later, Brie bolted free. "Drew, did you hear that?"

"Yeah. Shh... listen," he said, gently placing his finger to her lips.

Both of them stopped stone-still and listened for the slightest human sound. And when they heard the faint voice of someone calling for help, their eyes met.

In an instant, Drew's shoulders were erect. "It's the trapper," he exclaimed.

"Come on," he said, grabbing Brie by the forearm and hurrying her forward. Brie climbed into the boat and tried her best to stay out of Drew's way as he scrambled to the rear and got the motor cranked. Within seconds he had them heading back around the bend.

The trapper was lying on the ground when they got to him. His skin looked clammy, and his breathing was labored. But, somehow, he'd managed to pull up one leg of his dungarees. "I been snake-bit," he cried out to them.

Brie's eyes automatically dropped to the bare leg and, sure enough, she saw two small puncture marks about five inches above his ankle. The actual realization that he'd been bitten by a snake made her sick to her stomach. She felt almost dizzy.

"It was a moccasin," he grumbled.

"Is that poisonous?" she heard someone with her voice ask.

"Very," came Drew's reply.

After a moment, she looked up and saw that he had already gotten the first-aid kid from their boat. "Sit up, if you can," he said to the trapper as he placed his arm around the middle of the man's back and helped him come up. "You need to keep your heart elevated higher than the bite. It keeps the poison from spreading as fast."

Brie took a deep breath as she felt the world come back into focus again. She dropped to her knees. "I can help," she said steadily.

Drew immediately went to work placing a tourniquet above the bite and instructing Brie that she was to loosen it for a few seconds at regular minute intervals. Then he took a sharp razor from a sterile vial in the first-aid kit and made two tiny parallel slits across each fang mark. Using the suction syringe provided in the kit, he began to suction out as much poison as he could from the wound. He kept this up for several minutes.

"Ohh, man," the trapper moaned. "My leg burns like fire."

Drew's eyes met Brie's. "We've got to get him to a hospital."

"I got motor trouble," the trapper added in a weakening voice. "Can't use..." His voice trailed off.

Glancing back at their boat, Drew said, "Keep working the tourniquet like I told you, okay?"

Brie was much too anxious to even consider questioning any instructions he gave her. Besides, she certainly didn't know what was required of them in order to try to save this man's life. But, thank goodness, Drew obviously did. "Okay," she said, almost able to count every second as they ticked by from the enormous pulse beats she felt in her ears.

Drew darted off and returned in less than a minute. Together, they began their earnest struggle to get the stricken trapper to their boat. Drew carried most of the burden of the man's weight, but Brie handled what she could. When, they finally reached the boat, Brie realized that Drew had thrown their supplies onshore.

And from then on, all thoughts of finding their treasure before sunset were gone, replaced instead with the urgent need to try to save the life of another human being.

And as Drew gunned the outboard motor in the direction of help and Brie assured their sick, frightened patient that he would be all right, she looked up into Drew's worried gaze and began to have her first serious doubts concerning her earlier assumption of the man she had once had a crush on years ago.

Because, in that moment, one thing was crystal clear to her. Drew Naquin hadn't been thinking of himself when he'd instantly ditched his own mission to help out a total stranger who needed him. And no matter how she chose to analyze his actions today, she knew in her heart that they were in direct contradiction to the kind of man she had once thought him to be. So who was the *real* Drew Naquin?

Chapter Nine

Drew unlocked the back door to his apartment, reached inside and clicked on the light in the kitchen. Exhausted, Brie followed him inside.

"How about some coffee?" Drew asked, going straight for the cabinet where he kept a canister of ground coffee. "Something hot going down into the old stomach sure sounds good. I'm chilled to the bone."

"Me, too," Brie stated, dumping her shoulder bag on top of the counter. "The temperature must have dropped twenty-five degrees since night fell."

"Yeah," Drew agreed, getting the coffee brewing. "I wasn't even thinking of that possibility when I pitched out our coats from the boat along with all our other supplies. I was just thinking about that poor guy."

"I know," Brie said, pulling a chair out from the kitchen table and sitting in it. She sighed heavily. "Do you think he's going to be all right?"

"It's too soon to tell for sure, but the doctors at the hospital sounded hopeful."

"You helped save his life."

"No. *We* helped save his life. You did as much as I did."

"Did you notice how shaken his wife and kids were when they arrived?"

"Yeah. I couldn't help but feel sorry for them."

"Yeah, me, too," Brie said, crossing her arms on the table in front of her and slumping over until her head rested on them.

Within a few moments, Brie felt something—Drew's hands, she thought—on her shoulders, and, before she could even utter a sound, he began working his fingertips into her tired muscles. "Oh, God, but that feels good," she moaned.

No doubt about it. The man had hands to die for.

"It's too late to go after the treasure tonight," he said. "We'll start out again first thing in the morning."

"Umm . . . sounds good to me," Brie replied languorously, her eyes closed, her mouth spread in a simple smile.

And then she felt it. A kiss pressed ever so lightly against the back of her neck. The kiss was so slight that she wondered if she hadn't imagined it.

A moment later, she heard Drew say, "Coffee's ready." Her eyes sprang open. She *had* imagined it.

But, for a moment there, it certainly had felt real.

He poured coffee into two mugs, set Brie's mug down in front of her and then held out his own in a toast. "To us," he said, surprising her with a grin that sent her tummy rolling to the floor. "After all, this is our wedding night."

"So it is," Brie said, giddy with exhaustion and the recent memory of his fingertips massaging her shoulders. "Just don't get any crazy ideas," she added playfully.

"Who me?" Drew replied. "I would never think of doing such a thing."

They both took a sip of the coffee, then Drew settled in the chair next to her. "Now, tell me, how did a nice girl like you end up in a place like this?" He had that tummy-tingling grin on his face again.

Brie laughed. "Just damned lucky, I guess."

"Lady, I'd have to say the luck is all mine."

They continued smiling at each other as they sipped their coffee. Brie was very much aware of the change that had transpired in their relationship since they'd worked together in an attempt to save another human life. There was an affinity between them now. A oneness. At least, Brie felt it, and she wondered if he did, too.

"Bedtime," he said, giving her a moment to take her last swallow of coffee before carrying their empty mugs to the sink and setting them down inside. "This time you get the bed. I'll take the sofa—that is, unless you've changed your mind from last night and don't mind if we share the same bed."

Brie laughed. "I haven't changed my mind."

"You sure? Look, that's a big king-size bed upstairs, with plenty of room for two. And we're both so tired, it seems rather dumb for one of us to have to sleep on that miserable sofa."

"I don't mind sleeping on the sofa," Brie said, wanting to solve the problem of their sleeping arrangements as quickly as possible.

"No. If one of us has to sleep there, I insist that it be me," Drew said, walking into the next room and plopping himself onto the sofa. He pulled off his boots, and, after folding his hands behind his head, reclined against one end of it. "See. I fit perfectly."

"Your feet are hanging over the other end," Brie exclaimed.

"So," Drew said, turning on his side and bending his legs at the knees so that his whole frame was between the sofa's two armrests, "Now I fit."

"I insist on sleeping on the sofa," Brie persisted, placing her hands on her hips for emphasis.

He obviously wasn't impressed. "Good night, Brianna," he said, reaching up and clicking off the table lamp. The room was thrown into complete darkness. "Sleep tight."

"Ohh," Brie said, frustrated, "have it your way."

"No, my dear. We're having it your way, remember?"

There was a light on in the upstairs hall—thank goodness. Brie could see her way as she climbed each step. "Damn him, anyway," she mumbled under her breath. He was just trying to make her feel guilty. Manipulation, that's what it was. Pure manipulation.

And it was working.

Still . . . the thought of sleeping tonight on that sofa—or any sofa, for that matter—simply wasn't very pleasing. Her body ached with fatigue. Having a bed to rest in was definitely the better end of the bargain.

However, if she were going to be completely truthful with herself, what reason did she have for being so exhausted, especially in comparison to him? *He* was the one who had done all the work. True, she had helped out when she could. But for the most part, she'd been the observer. He'd been the soldier. Therefore, if she thought she was tired, just how exhausted must he feel?

She was on a guilt trip, all right, and the ride was all uphill.

Maybe she was being petty, she told herself as she undressed and then showered. Briefly she gave a thought to her long johns-style pajamas, which had undoubtedly been tossed out of the boat along with the other supplies. Either that, or they were in a box in the rear of Drew's truck. Regardless, she wasn't going to look for them. Instead, she found a clean T-shirt of his folded in a dresser drawer, quickly slipped it on over her head and then dived under the warm covers of his big, soft, comfortable bed.

Okay, she finally admitted to herself as she settled in, she *was* being childish about this whole thing. They were, after all, two consenting adults. Two consenting, *married* adults, at that. In fact, married to one another. Surely she wasn't going to be so prudish as to make him suffer through a long, uncomfortable night for propriety's sake. Even Mary Poppins wouldn't be that prudish.

Sighing in surrender a few moments later, Brie clicked on the bedside lamp, threw back the warm blankets covering her, jumped out of bed and tiptoed downstairs. She had no idea why she was tiptoeing. If he was going to come upstairs to bed with her—*she definitely didn't like the way that sounded*—then she was going to have to wake him up regardless. Still, she thought her sneak approach best.

She stopped just before reaching the sofa. "Drew, I've changed my mind," she whispered. Then she waited for his reply. When none came, she repeated what she'd said, only louder this time. Still, she heard nothing. Finally, she stepped closer and shook him. "Drew, are you awake?"

"Huh...? Ah, yeah—sure—I'm awake. Who could get to sleep this quick on this uncomfortable thing?"

"Look, I've changed my mind. I think we're adult enough to sleep in the same bed without, uh, without either of us getting any wrong ideas. Don't you?" Brie could barely see in the dark, but there was no mistaking the exact moment when she saw him spring up from the sofa.

"Sure, I do," Drew agreed, standing right in front of her.

Not knowing what else to say, Brie turned and plodded back upstairs. Drew followed right behind.

Entering his bedroom, she went to one side of the bed and stood at its edge. He went to the other and climbed in under the covers. Then he looked at her and grinned. "I really do like the way my T-shirt fits your tight little body." Then he flipped over on his side and said, "Nighty-night."

"Ohh!" Brie stated, knowing full well why he'd said what he had. T-shirts were notorious for clinging. She climbed in on her side of the bed, making sure she was near the edge, turned off the light and pulled the covers up under her chin. *Nighty-night, indeed!*

It seemed to Brie that she would never wake up, no matter how hard she tried to pull herself free from her dream. It was the same dream as always, the one where she ran after a tall man who walked faster and faster until she lost sight of him. In the dream, the man always turned around once so that she could see his face. However, often, when he did, he hadn't any face, and Brie somehow knew that on that particular night, the faceless man represented the father she'd never seen. But on most nights, she knew the man in her dream symbolized her grandfather, and the young girl desperately trying to catch up with him was none other than herself. And—oh—yes . . . she'd almost forgotten. Several times over the past nine years, the man had represented Drew.

Brie hated the dream and continued to strive to come awake from it. She tossed and turned and groaned and moaned in agony at being trapped within her own nighttime imaginings.

Suddenly she felt someone gently pulling her into his arms and whispering sweet nothings in her ear. It was someone with a voice as smooth as silk, with an embrace as comforting as a mother's womb. And somehow Brie knew this someone was going to make her life all better.

The tip of his tongue was warm, moist as it traced the outline of her ear. Ultimately he began nipping and pulling and sucking on her earlobe. Brie heard her own sharp intake of breath. She felt as if she were on fire.

The man in her dream was no longer in sight. Only Brie didn't care about him anymore, anyway. She knew instinctively that the man of her dreams—her soul mate— was finally at her side and that her body was now pressed against his. She knew it was his hands that had begun to explore her most intimate parts and she yearned with a fiery passion for him to give her complete fulfillment. So it didn't come as a surprise to her that, when he took her lips with his and eased her pliant body beneath his, she surrendered. And as her lover whispered of his agonizing need for her, Brie's heart and soul joined with his in a sensuous dance. Together, as one—as man and wife—they played out the oldest, sweetest love song of all time. It was the most wonderful dream Brie had ever had. Only she was awake now and she knew she hadn't been dreaming. No dream, no matter how real, or how wonderful it seemed, could have left her feeling so complete as a woman. She had just given her virginity to the man she loved, and she hadn't one single regret.

And when at last she stirred again, it was his lips that quieted hers with a kiss, and his throaty whispers that calmed her awakening spirit, so that a peaceful sleep unlike anything she had ever known finally overtook her.

Drew, however, couldn't fall asleep. Somehow, without his being aware of it, he had been slowly seduced into loving Brie. Who knew, maybe it had been Old Duke's wishes all along; or maybe it was simply destiny, showing him it held the winning hand, after all. Either way, no matter. Whoever, or whatever, had willed his and Brianna's union had known his deepest needs, even when he hadn't.

And judging from the way Brie had made love with him tonight, her needs were identical to his. True, she hadn't said as much during their intimacy. But then, he didn't need a degree in psychology to figure out that her trembling body was an indication of her passion for him. She *had* needed him, just as he had needed her. He could see now they belonged together. Undoubtedly, she would, too.

Content with the idea that he and Brianna would somehow work through their differences first thing in the morning and come to the same conclusion about their futures, Drew tightened his arm around his bride and, with his face curled in the softness of her hair, fell into a deep, restful sleep.

It was just before sunrise when Brie awoke with a start and, within seconds, recalled everything—Drew, their lovemaking—and knew without a doubt that none of last night had been a dream. Now the warm, tender sweetness they'd shared in the darkness of night was going to have to face the cold hard reality of day. And for Brie, nothing looked quite the same.

She knew instinctively that just because Drew hadn't resisted what was there in his bed for his taking didn't mean anything. Certainly, it didn't prove that he loved her. He'd said only that he needed her. A big difference. In fact, with all the endearing words that had come from him while she'd been in his arms, those three in particular had never been mentioned. The undeniable truth was he hadn't wanted her nine years ago when she'd thrown herself into his unwilling arms. And, since her arrival in Louisiana, he'd made it quite clear to her that he still didn't want her. At least, not for keeps. Obviously, last night had been a fluke. He'd just taken pity of the weak, love-starved woman he thought she was and had decided to give her a night of unforgettable sex. Everyone knew that men were quite capable of doing that sort of thing. They considered it a favor to a lonely woman.

Well, pity of any kind was the one thing she couldn't tolerate from anyone. But especially not from Drew.

She had to get up. Get away from him—now.

After a moment of indecision, Brie gently removed Drew's arm from around her and quietly slipped from his bed. For a moment she stayed there, barely breathing in the semidarkness while she stared down at him and memorized every detail of his features, from his dark brown tousled hair, to his full, slightly parted lips, to his day-old beard that now darkened his chin. She wanted to remember the smell of him, the taste of him, the way he'd made her feel when, together, they'd reached that pinnacle in their lovemaking. This night would stay a part of her forever.

She loved him. She'd known that for a long time now. But a one-sided love affair was not enough. Somewhere, in the not-so-distant future, a small part of her would come to hate him for not loving her in return, and she didn't think she could live with herself if that happened.

With a soft sigh and a sudden determination, Brie turned, walked quietly from the room and went downstairs. It would be daylight soon. If she hurried, there was time before Drew woke up to get her original belongings from the rear of his pickup truck, call a cab and head for the nearest airport that was capable of booking her on an immediate flight back to Atlanta. Even if accomplishing this meant she would have to hire a taxi to drive her all the way to New Orleans, she was getting out of here—immediately. She had come to Louisiana without anything but her pride, and she was going back to Georgia with little else. But if she stayed here a moment longer, even that would be in danger. And that was why she had to get away from Drew. He had within the palm of his hand the ability to cause her more heartache than she'd ever thought possible.

After calling a cab, she hung up the telephone in the kitchen and then slipped out the back door, closing it quietly behind her.

She didn't really blame Drew for what had happened between them. After all, she had wanted him as much as he had desired her. In fact, maybe, even more. After all, she reminded herself as she wiped away the sudden tears that sprang to her eyes, she was the one in love with him.

She *had* made a mistake in coming here. But her biggest mistake was in thinking that her grandfather had caused her her greatest heartache. Unfortunately, Drew Naquin would be the man who would hold that tragic title.

Call it foolish, but she still hoped when he went into the Atchafalaya Swamp today to look for his treasure, that he found a bountiful one awaiting him. But, either way, it would all be his to keep. He'd earned it. She didn't want a dime. No amount of silver and gold would ever heal her broken heart.

Drew knew something was wrong the moment he opened his eyes. It wasn't only that Brie wasn't cradled in his arms. She could have been in the bathroom taking a shower, or downstairs, fixing breakfast. But she was in neither place, and he knew it. She had left him.

He could feel it.

In his bones. In his gut. In his soul. It seemed to holler in protest as the reality of her leaving him settled in, deep down. The truth was, he would probably never see her again.

Her smell still lingered in the room—on his sheets, his pillow, all over his body.

He could still see her face in that moment—that magical, magical moment when they had been as one—her eyes closed ... her head thrown back ... her back arched. They had been man and wife in that moment. Married.

She'd left him, anyway. He'd laid himself on the line for her last night. He'd given in. He'd said he needed her. Hell, he hadn't said that to anyone since he was a kid. In fact, he'd told her that he desired her in a way he'd never before desired anyone. And still, it wasn't enough. What more did she want from him?

He had known this was how it would turn out. It was the way it always turned out when you let someone into your world. He had known she would expect more of him. Well, the truth was he'd given her his all. If she had wanted more, well, she was out of luck.

Drew rolled over on his side and then got out of bed. After all, he had a promise to keep to his old friend, and by this afternoon he would have fulfilled it. Then, tomorrow, after having found Brianna's inheritance, he would give the bounty to Samuel Jacobs and leave it up to the attorney to handle all the details, including contacting Brie so that she could receive what was rightfully hers. And then he would get on with his life.

It was what he had wanted for himself in the beginning. Only now, now that he knew what love was, the thought of carrying on alone, without Brie at his side, seemed rather fruitless. Something he'd never missed before was now missing from his life, and as a result he would never be the same again.

For the first time ever, Drew found himself wanting to put down roots.

But after finding and then losing the one person who could have made those roots grow and flourish in love, the knowledge that he had also lost his thirst for adventure came as no big surprise. It seemed he'd made it full circle since his childhood days as a liability to the state. He'd had nothing back then, and he had nothing now. And before he realized what was happening to him, Drew found a haunting loneliness—similar to the one he'd suffered from as a youth—seeping into his soul. He began to regret the choices he'd made for himself years ago when he had been young and foolish and thought of himself as invincible.

No man was invincible. There was good and bad. Heaven and hell. Life and death. And suddenly, he found he wanted to live his life so that when his time came to leave this world, he would leave behind something good of himself. His children. His love. His legacy.

It was so simple. Why hadn't he been able to see the whole picture before now?

But the problem for him was that he'd really screwed things up badly when he hadn't told Brie the three words he'd known she needed to hear when she'd made love with him. At the time it had seemed unnecessary. In fact, until this very moment, he hadn't wanted it to *be* necessary. Was it too late now to tell her of his change in heart?

God, he prayed not.

Brie received the telephone call from Samuel Jacobs on her second day back at work. Realizing that there was likely some additional paperwork to be done concerning the house and property she'd inherited from her grandfather, she wasn't surprised to hear his voice.

He began by telling her that Drew had found the treasure indicated on the map her grandfather had willed to them. It was a small metal box, he said, containing a single key and a note explaining in a certain code that only Drew could understand that the key opened a safe-deposit box at one of the local banks in Lafayette. Acting as Duke Bernard's power of attorney, he and Drew had opened the safe-deposit box and discovered there was two hundred thousand dollars in cash inside.

Brie was astounded at the news. *Two hundred thousand dollars? That was quite a find.* But she wasn't nearly as astounded as she found herself moments later when Samuel Jacobs continued to explain to her the whole underlying story surrounding her grandfather's will. Drew, it seemed, had suspected her grandfather of burying her inheritance and making out his will as he had in order to get rid of her fiancé, Carl Winthrop.

For the next few minutes, Jacobs had given her detail upon detail. By the time she hung up with him, Brie was in complete shock, having discovered that her grandfather's motives for writing his will as he had had been purely unselfish and that Drew's motives for going after the treasure were the same. For the first time in her life, she knew that her grandfather *had* cared for her. In fact, knowing he had gone out into the swamp alone to bury that key, enduring the kind of physical pain he must have in order to do so, made her weep.

And Drew. What was she to think of him?

He'd intimidated her. He'd lied to her. He'd married her... and all for the sole purpose of keeping his promise to her grandfather. He was, it seemed, a man of integrity, after all.

But then, she had come to know that, before she'd left Louisiana, on her own.

If only he could have said the words she'd needed to hear. It would have made all the difference in the world. Those three little words could have changed the outcome of their lives forever.

Still, Brie felt she needed to express her gratitude to him. After all, it was the least she could do. Especially after the sacrifices he'd made on her account. Why, he'd even gone so far as to give her his name.

But she wasn't strong enough yet to actually endure the agony of hearing his voice, so calling him was most definitely out of the question. Her heart was still too hurt just yet. She might start crying, and that would just kill her if she did.

She decided, instead, to write him a letter, thanking him for everything in a nice, cordial manner. She'd keep it short, simple and to the point. In essence, it would read, *Thank you, but no thank you. I don't need your pity.* Anyway, she felt certain he'd get her message, and that was the important thing.

His response to her letter arrived at her office twelve days after she'd mailed her thank-you note. It was accompanied by twelve long-stemmed burgundy-red roses and a small jewelry-size box that resembled a treasure chest. With trembling fingers Brie opened the box to find a small handwritten note that read:

I'm making roots. I need you. Please come home where you belong. You're the only treasure of my life.

Love,
Drew

Immediately, her heart swelled to enormous proportions and she felt she would explode with happiness. Within seconds, her fellow co-workers were peeking over her shoulders, wanting to see what was causing her so much elation. They knew roses were, undoubtedly, an exciting, romantic gift to receive, but Brie's reaction went far beyond the norm.

It was then that a release of her emotions came in the form of tears. In fact, she cried so much that her boss gave her the rest of the day off so that she could go home and get some badly needed rest. No one in her office would have understood if she had told them that home for her was four state lines away. And that rest for her would be an impossible achievement until she was back in Drew's arms, this time forever.

When Brie got back to her apartment, she didn't call Drew to tell him her plans to return—she would have cried even more if she had. Besides, she wanted the moment of her return to be a surprise for him. So, instead, she began to pack up her belongings and make the final arrangements necessary for leaving town.

Her best friend cried at the news of her leaving, but Brie made her promise to come to visit soon, describing the Cajun men she'd seen in Louisiana as the best-looking males on earth. Brie knew that was a sure way of getting her friend moving in any direction.

And when she told her employer her plans, he sent her on her way with his blessings and a letter of recommendation for future job interviews without insisting she give him the usual two-week job termination notice he required of his employees. He said that she had been a productive part of his company for five long years and wanted to show her his appreciation. Her last day at the office ended up being teary-eyed for everyone, including her boss.

And now she was on board the airplane that would take her home . . . back to her beloved, where she belonged.

Brie hired a taxi to drive her straight to Drew's apartment, where she was disappointed to discover he wasn't at home. Somehow, though, she knew in her heart that he wasn't far away. Not giving much thought to her next decision, she gave the cabdriver the address to her family homestead and told him to take her there.

When they reached the clearing where her ancestral home stood, the first thing she saw was Drew's red pickup truck, and her heart went bonkers. She paid for her ride, lifted her small suitcase—a moving service would be coming in two days with the rest of her belongings—and climbed out. The taxi soon disappeared down the narrow road leading away from the old house.

Brie watched where she stepped as she approached the front porch and entered the house. The first room was empty, but she could hear hammering and scuffling going on in another room at the back of the house. Drawing her eyebrows together in confusion, she arrived in the doorway of that room and saw Drew standing with his face to the wall. He had a hammer in one hand and a nail in the other. She saw him lift the hammer and bring it down on the nail, correction, on his fingernail. He howled and then let out a short string of low curses.

"Tsk—tsk," Brie said from behind him. "That's no way for a true carpenter to behave. Haven't you ever heard of the number one rule of survival?"

By this time, Drew had turned around in shock and was staring at her as if she were a ghost. Brie smiled at him. "Hi."

After his moment of astonishment, Drew's expression became serious. "Why did you come, Brie?"

Noting the hint of anger in his voice, Brie hesitated. "I—I came because I thought you wanted me to."

A slow, sexy grin began to spread across Drew's face as he started moving toward her. "Oh, God, Brie, I've been waiting these past couple of days to hear from you. I was beginning to fear you weren't going to come."

And then she was in his arms and he was kissing her and she was kissing him back. "I love you, woman. Don't you ever leave me again."

"I won't," Brie replied, looking into his soulful eyes, searching for the promise she needed to hear from him.

"Brie, honey, I know you're afraid to trust in me. After all I've said about my not wanting to settle down, I can't say I blame you. But I'm not your father, or your grandfather. I'm not even the same guy who once thought he was invincible. I know now I'm not invincible, and the thought of going through life without you is downright scary. I need you, and, if you'll give me half a chance, I'll prove it every single day of my life. But for now, all I can do is promise to be right here at your side forever."

"Is this another one of those promises, like the one you made on my grandfather's Bible?" she asked with a twinkle in her eyes, recalling the details of the story Samuel Jacobs had relayed to her during their last telephone conversation.

"You betcha, it is," he replied, happily. He gestured for her to examine the room where they stood. "Look, I'm making roots."

For the first time, Brie really looked around the room and that was when she realized that he had already begun to renovate the old house. "What are you doing?"

"Fixing up our home. I know you love this place...
and...well, I figure we can use it for a while—until the
babies start coming—and then we'll build us a bigger
house right next door and use this one as our honeymoon
cottage. What do you think?"

"Babies?" Brie asked.

He nodded. "Several. I think this family needs to do
some growing. That is, if it's all right with you."

"It's my dream-come-true."

Suddenly she was in his arms again. "Brie, honey, I
want to try to make all your dreams come true."

She smiled at him. "You already have."

Then he kissed her long and hard.

And when it ended, he took her by the hand and began
to pull her along behind him. "Come on, I have something I want to show you."

"What?"

He turned and placed his finger across her lips. "No
questions asked, okay?"

Remembering the way she had questioned him before
about every little detail, she laughed. "Okay."

She followed him out of the house and down a long path
that led through the dense woods. It took them a while to
reach the other side, and Brie was somewhat awed when
she realized they had arrived on the back side of the small
cemetery where her grandfather was buried. They went to
his grave and on it Brie placed the gold chrysanthemum
she'd found in an overgrown flower garden near the old
house and then prayed a silent prayer for him, now knowing in her heart that he *had* cared for her.

"Over here," Drew was saying as she lifted her head. He
took her hand once more and led her on a weaving path
between graves until they came to a dogwood tree about a
hundred feet away.

"Look," he said, stopping beneath it.

"What?" Brie asked, still not understanding what he was showing her.

"Read the inscriptions on these graves, Brie," he said, gesturing with the tilt of his chin to a couple of stones that were at their feet.

Brie immediately glanced down at the name engraved on the first headstone and then she swung her eyes over to the one right next to it. Drew had found her great-grandparents' grave site, and they were indeed buried just as she had imagined them, side by side, together for all time, their union in this life entombed for all future generations to see.

In that moment, Brie felt as though her treasure chest of dreams had surely been found and opened, and she was now reaping the benefits.

She knew she would always have regrets about her estranged relationship with her grandfather. In fact, she would have gladly given all the money he'd willed her for just a few minutes with him. But that was never to be and she had to come to terms with that.

She looked up at Drew with tears in her eyes. "You've made me so happy today."

He placed his arms around her and kissed her passionately, right there in the small cemetery for all souls, living and dead, to see. "Today—*every* day of my life—I plan to make you happy. It's a promise, my darling, that I'll always keep. I love you, Brie."

"I love you, Drew. I've loved you for a long time."

"We're going to be so happy here," he replied, smiling into her glistening eyes. "You and me, digging in with our roots...making our home a house of love for us and our children and our children's children."

"We're going to have a wonderful life. With ups and downs—but with lots of love," Brie replied, smiling up at him.

And as they turned and slowly walked away, side by side, hand in hand, Brie thought she could hear the soft whispers of her ancestors in the cool evening breeze, welcoming her home—at last.

Epilogue

One Year Later
The Atchafalaya Basin Swamp

Drew wiped the sweat from his forehead as he dug the shovel deeper into the soft earth. Last year at this time, the weather was cool. Today, it was hot.

But Drew didn't care. He and Brie—and their unborn child—were out here together, and that was all that mattered to him. Again, he pushed the shovel deeper into the ground. Finally he looked up at Brie, who sat nearby in a folding lawn chair and asked if she thought the hole he'd dug was deep enough.

"It isn't a very big chest," she said, sitting with her legs crossed and sipping from a bottle of flavored water. She took a moment to lean forward and peek inside the opening in the ground. "I think that's plenty deep. What do you think?"

"I think so, too," Drew said, reaching for the small treasure chest she handed him. He placed it in the hole and covered it up with soil. "Now, that ought to do it."

"What are we going to do with the wine bottle?"

"We'll pitch it out into the water on our way back to the landing."

"Great!" Brie said excitedly. "I think this is so romantic, don't you?"

"Umm . . . more adventurous, I think," Drew added as he helped Brie get into their motorboat so they could head back before dark. "How's she doing?" he asked, momentarily placing his hand on her protruding stomach. From the beginning, he had wanted their first child to be a girl. He'd said it was because he had come to realize that women were stronger in nature than men, therefore, their baby girl would set a good example for any younger brothers that would follow. Brie thought he was full of hot air and always told him so—until her ultrasound had come back two days ago.

"*She* is doing just fine," Brie replied, quickly sitting herself down inside the rocking boat. They were going to name their first child after her grandmother.

In a few moments, Drew had them heading for home. But about two miles from shore, he slowed the motor down to a crawl and lifted a corked wine bottle containing a map inside. After giving his wife a playful wink, he pitched it out into the water as far as he could.

"Someday, someone is going to find that map," Brie said laughingly. "And they're going to think a pirate's lost fortune is awaiting them."

"Well, it is a fortune," Drew replied. "A fortune of good advice."

They smiled knowingly at each other as the map to the treasure they'd just buried drifted farther and farther away from them. After a few moments, Drew gunned the motor and their boat sped off in the direction of home. Neither of them bothered to look back.

And if...somehow...someday...somewhere...that wine bottle were ever found and the map inside taken seriously, it would lead the adventurous treasure hunter to a small chest buried two feet under the ground beneath an old willow tree. And inside the chest, he or she would find a note that read:

Go home to your beloved. True love is the only treasure worth seeking.

* * * * *